The Reeducation of
Savannah McGuire

THE REEDUCATION OF SAVANNAH MCGUIRE

© 2015 HEIDI MCLAUGHLIN

COVER DESIGN: Sarah Hansen at Okay Creations

EDITING: Traci Blackwood

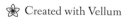 Created with Vellum

Chapter One

Tyler

*S*avannah McGuire, the girl who was taken from Rivers Crossing years ago by her power-hungry mother, is due to return. I'm excited and nervous, a deadly combination. Diagnosis: pure anxiety. My palms are sweaty, my leg is bouncing up and down and I don't know why. Sure, it's been five years since we've seen or spoken to each other, but her coming back here shouldn't make me feel like I'm about to go on a date with Miss America.

When I see the old Greyhound bus come rumbling down the road, I straighten in my seat, clutching the steering wheel until my knuckles are white with tension. I've known about her return for a week now, but haven't let the news set in that my one-time best friend is returning. Half of me thought this day would never happen because something would prevent her from coming home. I'm still not convinced that it will be her getting off the bus in a few seconds.

The Greyhound comes to a halt, its brakes squealing from the pressure. The door swings open and my eyes instantly scan the windows to see if I can spot Savannah. I hold my breath when I see candy-apple-red heels hitting the last step before reaching the cracked pavement. Her long blonde hair sways lightly from the exhaust blowing behind her. It's stifling out and this is as much of a breeze as she's going to get. She moves her head back and forth just like those stupid hair commercials my mom is always watching. She looks up and down the road before setting her hands on her hips. I shake my head, knowing that this ain't my Savannah.

The bus isn't pulling away so I know Savannah is still on it. I lean into the steering wheel to get a better look. The blonde side steps and allows the next passenger off the bus. This is my Savannah, with her shoulder-length brown hair and oversized clothes. She was always wearing her Uncle Bobby's shirts when we were younger, afraid of how her body was changing. Jeremiah used to call her Mouse, and he'll be happy to see that she hasn't changed.

After throwing my shoulder into the door, I hop out and clap my hands once out of excitement. I rush over to Savannah and pick her up, twirling her around. "God, I've missed you. Are you ready to have the best summer of your life?"

"Uh, put me down, please."

Fulfilling her request, but not ready to let go, I pull her into a hug. Her hands push firmly against my chest as she steps away. Savannah brushes off her clothes as if I've contaminated them. The blonde clears her throat and smiles. I roll my eyes. I know it's probably real hard for her to stand here and watch this reunion, but it's not my fault that her family isn't here on time. By her looks, I'm sure she gets all the attention she wants.

"Are you ready to go, Savannah?"

"Yes, I am." The blonde speaks up. I look at her. With her hand on her hip, she taps her toe on the ground and smirks.

"Look ma'am, I'm sorry your kinfolk aren't here to get ya and if ya want we can wait, but I'm sure they'll be along soon." I reach for Savannah's bags, but her hand stops me.

"I don't know you," she says quietly as she removes my hand from her suitcase.

"Excuse me?" I question, as I stand tall. "What do you mean you don't know me?"

She shrugs. "I don't know you and my name's not Savannah."

"Mine is though, and just wait until I tell my Uncle Bobby how you tried to take someone else home, Tyler King."

Slowly turning and eyeing the statuesque blonde, my heart stops beating. The smirk is back, or it never left. I step closer so I can see what happened to the mousy brunette I used to know. Her gaze follows mine and I look her over. She's taller, leaner and, besides the obvious hair color change, looks nothing like she did when she left here. Her teeth are straight and missing the metal that used to clog her mouth. There's no way this woman is only seventeen years old.

I swallow hard and break eye contact. This ain't gonna be good. When I thought she was this other girl, I pictured us hanging out. Now that I'm looking at her, the hanging out idea doesn't seem to be the best thing for me.

One thing's for sure: New York did a number on my Savannah.

"Wow, Savannah."

She nods, pursing her lips. "It's Vanna," she informs me as she stalks past me toward my truck. I follow her and mentally scold myself when my eyes fall on her cotton-covered ass. The mousy-non-Savannah mocks me in disgust. I run my hand over the back of my neck and sigh.

"Sorry 'bout that," I say. "Um... do you need a ride?"

She shakes her head and I deduce that I'm better off just leaving her. I've already embarrassed her and myself enough to last us a lifetime. I pick up Savannah's bags and hustle back to the truck. I have a feeling it's gonna be one long summer and once her Uncle Bobby sees her he's gonna flip. She's going to be every man's wet dream in a forty-mile radius and I just know I'm going to be tasked with taking care of her. Just call me the glorified babysitter of the mousy farm girl turned New York socialite.

I remember the day she left. I thought her momma was joking when she said they were moving, so when they packed their bags and got into the car, I was left standing there, stunned. I was so hurt that I refused to say good-bye. We didn't promise to write or even call each other. We were too young for those types of commitments. Watching her being driven away from me is my most vivid memory and one that has been replaying in my mind for the past week.

I was fifteen when she left. We'd grown up together, attending the same school, church and having Sunday suppers on her uncle's wrap-around porch. Our mommas always joked that we'd end up married to each other as soon as she turned eighteen and we'd start spitting out babies. After a while, I just believed them. It seemed like destiny. That was until my teenage hormones kicked in, and when I discovered girls, Savannah wanted nothing to do with me. She caught me a time or two with my hands in places they shouldn't have been and each time she'd just pretend like nothing was happening.

Even though our mommas wanted us to get married, there is an age difference between us and I matured faster. Savannah was quiet and shy, never really showing any interest in anything but her horse. Living in a small town, people have expectations and there was one on her and me, but it wasn't like I could take her out on a date or anything. Looking at her now, I wish I could've.

I climb into the cab of my truck and pull the door shut. She jumps in and clutches her purse tightly to her body. I let my hand dangle over the steering wheel thinking about all the things I want to say to her. Right now the only thing forming is the idiotic sentence of "damn, you grew up", but I have a feeling that will earn me a slap and I'd rather save that for later in the barn. I instantly chide myself for thinking I'll get her to the barn like that. She just got here and I'm sure she has a rich pretty boy waiting on her back home.

"Hello, Savannah. Long time no see." She adjusts slightly, turning farther away from me, and stares out her window. Her mood has changed from somewhat friendly to icy cold. I don't blame her. The warm reception I gave the other woman was probably what she was expecting and didn't get.

"It's Vanna."

I want to laugh at how straight-laced she sounds but hold back. Something tells me she's turned into a spitfire and that would be the spark to set her off. I've already pissed her off enough for one day. Her uncle said something about her getting into trouble one too many times at school and that her momma is too busy with her job to keep her under control. Apparently the answer was to send her back to where she got her start, even if she's not going to fit in around these parts anymore.

"Savannah," I reply purposely. There's no way in hell I'm calling her Vanna after that middle-aged letter turner that my grandma watches nightly.

She huffs, but doesn't say anything. I get the impression that she's used to getting her way, especially with men. Sadly for her, life doesn't work like that in these parts.

"How far 'til my uncle's house?"

I look out the windshield, pretending I need to gauge the distance. I shrug. "Twenty minutes or so."

"Well, shouldn't we get moving?"

I shake my head and mentally kick my own ass for how this day has started. I'd like a redo, please. Hell yeah I'd jump out of this truck and scoop her up in my arms if I knew what she had grown into, but I was remembering my reserved Savannah, not the model sitting next to me.

Cranking my key to start the engine, I'm happy for the loud roar to drown out my thoughts about her and us... in the barn. It's never gonna happen so I just need to stop thinking about it. I need to remember mud pie, cow tippin' and catching lightnin' bugs.

"Hang on tight, sweetheart." I press down on the gas as I throw my truck into drive. She slams back against the seat, her door barely closed. I'm trying not to laugh but her high-pitched squeal is cracking me up. She's turned into such a girly girl that someone is going to have to break her out of it and it ain't gonna be me.

Chapter Two

Savannah

$\mathcal{M}$y hair is blowing in all kinds of directions as the deathtrap I'm stuck in barrels down the road. I don't see the automatic window lever and I refuse to acknowledge or even look at Tyler. He forgot who I was! How does that happen? I haven't changed that much and you would think that when I'm smiling at him like a freaking buffoon he would know it's me. Who forgets their supposed best friend? The moron beside me does, that's who.

I look over at Tyler to find him smiling. With the way my luck has been going this past month, he's probably remembering some horribly disgusting moment in my pre-teen life that he's all too happy to drudge up at the most inopportune time. Like when I'm hitting on my uncle's ranch-hand. I overheard my mom asking my uncle Bobby about his ranch-hand, leading me to believe she doesn't want me near him. She took me out of school, refusing to let me finish out my senior year because her parenting skills blow, so I'm going to do what I can to entertain myself. I need some excitement in my life and if that comes in the form of a guy I'll never see again, so be it.

His left arm hangs out the window while the other rests on top of the steering wheel. At some point in my attempt to ignore him, he's put on a hat and aviators cover his eyes. Chicks dig aviators. Who knew someone like him could actually wear something fashionable? I look away, not willing to get caught staring. I don't want him to think I'm interested, because I'm not. I don't care if he's good looking with his tanned arms and defined muscles. So what if his shirt stretches across his chest and I can see the outline of his pectoral muscles? He made me look like a crazed fool standing there at the bus while he doted on that other girl.

My head falls against the door as I take in the passing scenery. I don't want to be here. I've made my thoughts on the idea of spending my summer here loud and clear. No one was listening, least of all my mother who has it in her head that I'm some type of juvenile delinquent. One incident and I'm slapped with a label. She's not exactly a good example of a perfect parent. Once I started high school, I was left to figure shit out on my own. I suppose when you're one of the most sought after divorce attorneys in New York City, you put your job before your family and forget that it's dinner time or your daughter's dance recital. Truth be told, if my mom knew half the shit I've done, she would've sent me out here a long time ago. Getting caught was never in the plans. Who knew she'd finally decide to come home early?

My mom is being unreasonable though. Every kid experiments; it's a part of life. My punishment shouldn't be finishing out my senior year and spending my summer in a Podunk town away from my friends, shopping and any vice I need to numb my wandering thoughts on the miserable life I have.

We turn down another dirt road and my uncle's ranch comes into view. My mom said I loved it here when I was a kid, always running around barefoot and catching frogs down at the pond. The thought makes me shudder as I look at my freshly manicured toes. I do believe my mother laughed when I asked about manicure and pedicure services and said something on how I'm nothing but a spoiled brat who needs a lesson in life. Of course my eyes rolled. She raised me, so if I'm spoiled it's because of her childrearing abilities, not because of me.

The truck comes to a stop and idles in the driveway. By the way Tyler looks right now, with his cheek pulled in, he's not getting out. That also means he's not going to help with me with my luggage so I'm going to have to do it myself. I sigh heavily and lift the handle to get out. The door doesn't budge. I try again, and nothing. Tyler, the asshole, starts to laugh before reaching across my legs and pushing the door open. The tingling I feel when his arm brushes across my leg leaves a burning sensation, as if glowing embers are resting on my skin. I look at him quickly, but he's focused on the house, not me. Everything in me is telling me that I need to say thank you, but I can't. The words aren't forming on my lips. I've never felt... tongue-tied?

I shake my head and slide out of the truck, but don't close the door until my suitcase is securely on the ground. Once I do, he's driving so fast out of the driveway that rocks are flying toward me. A few hit my legs and I cry out in pain, anger and frustration. There's no way I liked living here. It's dirty and nature makes my skin crawl.

"Well, well, well, if it ain't my little Savvy."

As much as I don't want to be here, I love my uncle. He's been a father to me for as long as I can remember. My dad passed away when I was two and I only remember him from pictures, but my memories of Uncle Bobby are fresh – well, as clear as they can be after being gone for so long. I smile as he comes stomping down the steps of his old farmhouse. It looks the same, but more modern and very clean. It warms my heart to know that he's kept it up all these years and didn't suffer in the recession like others.

"Hi, Uncle Bobby," I say as I wrap my arms around his neck. He picks me up and swings me around, earning him a girly squeal. This is what I would've done had Tyler been like this with me and not the other girl. But no, he had to make my homecoming awkward and remind me why I don't want to be here.

"How's my Savvy?" he asks as he sets me down.

I shrug, because I honestly don't know how I am. My life is a wreck and is only made worse by being here. I don't want to tell him that, but I'm sure he knows. He's always known. If it was a bump on my knee or a bee sting, Uncle Bobby had the cure. I don't know if he was making up for his brother, my father, not being able to be around or what, but he was the dad I needed until we moved away. I know I've changed and I suspect everyone else has, as well, but there are things that I hope are the same. If I'm feeling down, will he have homemade ice cream waiting for me? I'm hoping not because I'm down all the time and ice cream is the last thing I need right now. Uncle Bobby picks up my suitcase and takes my hand in his empty one, leading me to the house. The covered porch brings back memories of many dinners and camp outs I used to have with my mom. We lived here when I was younger because it was easier for everyone after my daddy died.

When I get inside I see that nothing - yet everything - has changed. My pictures from when I was little adorn the walls and the house still smells like home cooking, something that I can't get in New York. The aroma of freshly baked pie and a chicken roasting in the oven wafts through the walls. I inhale deeply, closing my eyes to try to bring up memories of running through the halls of this house. When I open them, I notice that the furniture is new and looks unbelievably comfortable. I can see myself getting lost while I watch this ranch hand work the land... hopefully with his shirt off. I step closer to the mantle and run my finger along the wood. Living in an apartment for so long, you forget how much love goes into building a home. An old picture catches my eye. It's of me and Tyler with our arms wrapped around each other. Both of us are covered in dirt and sweat, and he's holding a frog in his hand. We were so close and probably would still be if I hadn't been forced to move. When you're young and dependent upon others, what's important to you slips through your fingers. I thought of him until he just became a memory that I kept to myself. None of my private school friends cared about the stories I had to tell.

"Come on, there's someone in the kitchen who has missed her girl and is dying to see you."

I shuffle my feet into the kitchen to find my Aunt Sue hunched over the sink. She turns and gasps, covering her mouth as her eyes start to water. I fall into her arms and shed the tears that I had been saving for when I'd see her again. When we left, I begged my mom to bring us back to visit, but we never had any time. Her career was important to her and because of that I've lost time with my two favorite people.

"I'm so glad you're home," she says, cupping my face.

I nod, unable to find my voice. As happy as I am to see her and Uncle Bobby, I don't belong on a ranch. I belong in the city.

Chapter Three

Tyler

I slam my hand against my steering wheel to keep in time with the beat of the song blasting through my speakers. The need to hit something is prevalent and I haven't felt like this in a long time, not since I found my girlfriend Annamae - now my ex – playing "mow my lawn" with her momma's landscaper behind her garage. Nothing really prepares you to find your girlfriend like that. My fist knew what to do though. It was only after I beat the kid to a pulp that she proclaimed her love for him. With that I just laughed and walked away. My one-year of dating a Southern Belle went down the drain just like that. That wasn't a good day, but today, while shitty, ain't the same. The sudden onset of energy needs to be released and the only way I know how to do that is to find a punching bag or go ride the bull at Red's.

I don't know what I was expecting today, but that wasn't it. How could I not know that was Savannah standing there? I should've known. We're connected. I know we're all grown up now, but we were close. We were friends for a long time. Hell, I'd even seen her naked a time or two even though it was long before she was looking like she's looking now... and damn, is she fine now.

I pull into the dirt parking lot of Red's and shut off the engine. Not too many cars are here tonight, which is just perfect for me. This is the town's watering hole – for everyone. Red doesn't care. He's been serving minors for as long as he can remember, never afraid that the law will crack down on him. We're the epitome of Small Town America and that means the police chief is someone's daddy, uncle, brother or cousin and probably sitting at the bar with a cold one in his hand, not giving a rat's ass if some minor is in here. Just don't speed. If you're caught speeding, he'll bust your ass and make you pay a hefty fine. I never speed.

When I walk in, my best friend Jeremiah is leaning over a table full of girls getting his flirt on. I saddle up to an empty stool and tap on the bar. Della's working the bar tonight. She smiles and nods giving me the indication that she knows what I want. I look over my shoulder at Jeremiah and have to laugh. He's the town's poster boy for a redneck. He's always dressed in plaid with his big shiny belt buckle, cowboy hat and boots. The boy even walks like he just dismounted a bull and always has his thumbs in his pockets. He's who the Yankees make fun of. The chicks dig him though, especially the ones just passing through. They all think they've found themselves a real-life cowboy. They just don't know that he's a real-life horn dog too.

Jeremiah Moore is a man who can't form a proper sentence, unless you're a chick he's trying to pick up.

Then he becomes mister cool cat or whatever corny ass nickname he's given himself. He's articulate and smooth and the girls are putty in his hands. It makes me sick sometimes, but he's still my best friend and I know he'd do anything for me, as I would him. It still grates me that this oaf gets any chick he wants, yet I have to work my tail off for a little attention. It dawns on me that I have to keep Savannah away from him. Even though they know each other, he'll really want to get to know her now.

Red's is everything you want in a bar. It's open all week long, they serve the greasiest burgers in town, beer's always cold and the women are a-plenty. The bartenders know everything about everyone. There are so many peanut shells on the ground that it's a new type of flooring. Music's always playing and you're bound to find at least one of your friends hanging out. On the weekends there's dancing and a few bands stop through every now and again. Red even has a mechanical bull-riding contest once a year, and that brings in a lot of city folk. Red's is the place that those city girls like to escape to find their "cowboy". We don't mind. It's always nice having Southern Belles around.

The cold amber liquid feels good coating the back of my throat, but I don't have time to savor it as a slap on the back makes me spit and choke. I swipe the back of my hand across my mouth as I cough and regain my composure. Jeremiah sits down next to me, his own mug of beer resting in his hand.

"She here?" I look at him out of the corner of my eye and shake my head. His eyebrows are waggling up and down. He does that when he talks about any girl, but what he doesn't know is that Savannah McGuire is beautiful. What he also doesn't know is that I messed up the reunion and her attitude is less than friendly.

"Yeah, man, she's here." I chug the rest of my beer and set the mug on the bar, signaling for another one. I'm not about to sit here and get drunk, but the liquid definitely curbs my piss-poor attitude where she's concerned. "She arrived with legs that are a fucking mile long and she wears them damn high ass heels that we're always making fun of."

He looks at me questioningly. "Mousy?"

I nod and tip my mug back. "I wouldn't call her that though. She looks nothing like she did when she was twelve. Hell man, when she got off the bus, there was another chick with her and I thought that she was the other one. Mou... Savannah gave me such attitude that she ignored me all the way back to Bobby's."

"She smokin'?"

I nod, reluctantly. I don't want to think of her like that and I definitely don't want Jeremiah thinking of Savannah in that way, but damn it all to hell, she's the most gorgeous girl I've ever lain my eyes on.

Jeremiah laughs and slams his glass onto the bar. It's a good thing it's half empty; Della hates it when her bar gets messy. "So if she has legs for miles and she's smokin', why aren't they wrapped around your waist?"

I sigh out of frustration that I shouldn't feel. The thought of her and me like that overtakes my mind. Savannah and I didn't keep in touch. We weren't able to. To me, she was a friend that I was growing up with and teasing along the way from when she got braces, to when she'd come running into the house because we drenched her with water. She wasn't supposed to grow up and be beautiful. She was supposed to stay the same so we could

ation of Savannah McGuire

pick up where we left off. Now she's like that senior girl in high school that all the freshman boys had hard-ons for.

"Savannah..." Even saying her name overloads my senses. I had hoped she'd say "hi" to her aunt and uncle and we'd hop in my rig and come here to Red's to talk and hang out. "She doesn't belong here," I sigh with a hint of sorrow in my voice. I know I shouldn't care, but deep down I do. I'll wake up tomorrow, go to work and pretend that I'm not watching for her. When lunch rolls around, I'll opt to eat in the barn and stay far away from the house and Aunt Sue's cooking. I need to keep my distance and not let lines get crossed.

"Did you pick her up and spin her around like they do in the romance flicks?" Jeremiah's always watches movies to learn how to impress the girls. It works for him and maybe I should do the same, but by the way she was standing there all high and mighty, I think she would've handed my ass to me with her purse.

"That was my plan, but I picked the wrong girl up." I shake my head. "She stood there with this attitude and I was like, 'what' and she pointed out that she was Savannah and not the other girl who I kept calling Savannah. Then she goes and tells me to call her Vanna. Can you believe that shit?"

"I can't believe you picked up the wrong girl. That's some mean shit, Ty."

I shrug. "Yeah, well, she sure showed me what her big city attitude is like. Girl needs to remember where she came from."

Jeremiah laughs and beckons for a refill. "You gonna show her?"

I nod. "Bobby says she needs to work on the ranch. I guess she did some shit that her momma ain't too happy

7

with. Little Miss Savannah is gonna have to sling some shit."

"I'll be there to watch that. There's nothing like a fine ass chick bending over to pick up some manure." Normally I'd disagree with him, but knowing I'll be watching her get dirty is pretty exciting. "What'd'ya say we take these two behind me out and show them a good time?"

I look over my shoulder at the two girls behind us and wink. A good time is exactly what I need to get my mind off of Savannah.

Chapter Four

Savannah

*M*y eyes squint, trying to block out the bright sunlight beaming through the windows. I can't cover my face with a blanket or pillow because it's too damn hot and I'll suffocate. I'm going to have to ask Uncle Bobby to take me to town to buy some blackout curtains because I'm not going to be able to sleep once the sun rises.

I roll over toward the wall and open my eyes slowly. This was my room when I was little and nothing has changed. The bubblegum-pink walls are dull in color and in desperate need of being revived or painted a different color. My basket of My Little Ponies still sits in the corner from when I was seven. They were my most prized possessions and Tyler always tried to steal them from me. Why Aunt Sue kept them is beyond me. She had to know I was going to grow out of playing with plastic horses with multicolored hair. Unless Tyler still likes to play with them. That thought alone makes me giddy.

I can hear the dull buzz of a mower off in the distance. It's something I don't hear in the City unless I'm walking through Central Park or am at a friend's summer home. Can't say if I've missed that sound or not, around here it means work and that means Uncle Bobby and his ranch hands are already working the fields. Last night we didn't talk about what chores I'd have to do. If I had my way, the list would be non-existent. It's bad enough that I have to do homework and mail it in once a week. "Homeschooling" is what they called it when my mom was filling out the paperwork to send me here. It was the only option, because I refused to start a new school. If she's going to send me away, I'm going to make it difficult on her. I thought I had outsmarted her until she told me that I have to pass the rest of my classes with flying colors or I wouldn't be allowed to go to Paris in the fall, and I so want to go to Paris.

I throw back the sheet and blanket that's covering me. It's blazing hot and there's no air conditioner in my room. That's another thing I'm going to have to ask Uncle Bobby about. I don't know how anyone can sleep up here with this stifling heat. Sleep evaded me last night because of the humidity and the noises from the outside. I'm used to horns honking and sirens every half hour, people yelling and gunshots being fired, not crickets and coyotes howling at the moon. I don't want to be here and it's not because I don't love my aunt and uncle, it's because this place isn't for me. Maybe at one time I fit in, but that was another time. I've adapted, changed. I don't know anything about haying or working a ranch and I definitely don't have the necessary wardrobe to be here.

My feet touch the hardwood floor and I relish in the

cool feeling of the old wood. I could sleep on the floor. I could move my mattress down here or even sleep outside on the covered porch like I did many times when I was younger. Uncle Bobby never liked that though, and would sleep out there too, always afraid of a wanderer coming onto his land looking for a place to sleep or a day job to make some quick cash. No, I can't imagine he'd agree to me doing that now, not after what my mom told him.

As soon as I'm halfway down the stairs, the smell of freshly baked muffins makes my stomach growl. I haven't had a home cooked breakfast in years. Cold cereal or a bagel from the corner coffee shop is how I usually start my mornings. Lunch is cafeteria food or, if I'm feeling brave, the corner bodega when I shouldn't be leaving campus. Dinner is also a solo affair. We'd have random maids who made sure something frozen was available, but the sit down dinners we had after church when we lived here ceased to exist once we moved to New York.

"Mornin', Savvy," Aunt Sue calls out with her back facing me. I stand in the doorway and watch her for a moment. She's still as short as I remember. I used to ask Uncle Bobby how she could reach the top of the cupboards and he used to tease, saying that she was magic. It's the same magic that fixed me when I had the flu or my teddy bear had a rip that needed to be sewn. Part of me still wants to believe she's full of magic and can fix anything. Except for me, that is. According to my mom, I can't be fixed. I'm on the path to self-destruction and the only cure is going to come from hard manual labor.

The kitchen isn't like I remember. It seemed smaller when I was a kid, but now it's a large open space with a lot of natural light coming in. The counter tops that used to be robin's egg blue are now wood and shiny. The cabinets are white, but don't reach the ceiling. Resting on top of the cabinets are knickknacks and old mason jars. A huge bay window affords whoever is standing at the sink an opportunity to look out back. I used to have a swing set out there when I was little, but I'm sure that's long gone. I can barely see the top of the white picket fence that divides the yard from the pasture from where I stand. I have a feeling I'll be out there by lunchtime doing who knows what and complaining about it. Maybe if I'm lucky, my schoolwork will be the only chore I have to do.

"Good morning." She turns and smiles, until her eyes take in what I'm wearing. I cross my arms over my midsection and look away. Everyone is always judging.

Aunt Sue shakes her head. "You don't want to be dressing like that around here, missy."

"Why's that?" I ask, defiantly. No one has cared about the way I dress for as long as I can remember. Why should they start now? Even my very expensive private school mandated that we wear skirts and the ones that were issued were short. They dressed us like every pervert's fantasy. This is common attire for girls my age, a cami and boxers. Heck most of my friends wear less to bed.

"Them boys outside are girl crazy and you're ripe for the pickin'."

"I'm sure they're far too old for me, Aunt Sue."

"Mhm," she mumbles and turns back to the counter. "Uncle Bobby ain't gonna be too thrilled to see you waltzing around here with no britches on."

"These are my pajamas. What am I supposed to do, come down dressed to the nines every morning?"

She turns around and wipes her hands on her apron. Every memory I have of her is in this kitchen. Aunt Sue cooks for everyone and for every occasion. "Now, no one says you have to be gussied up for breakfast, just covered is all."

I try not to roll my eyes, but I can't help it. Everyone has something to say about me, whether it's my grades, the way I dress or what I do in my free time. I pick up the carton of orange juice and pour myself a glass before walking to the window and looking out. It looks gorgeous outside and I can see myself lying out in the sun today, catching some rays.

My glass stalls at my lips as Tyler walks past. He doesn't look my way, but stops by the window and yells at someone. I set down my juice and watch him. He takes off his hat and wipes his sweat with his forearm. I don't know if Tyler is the guy my mom slipped up about or not, but he's definitely giving me pause. Not that I'd let him in on that little fact. I lean forward as he pulls the neck of his shirt over his head. The muscles in his back move in fluid motion and all I can think is that guys do not look like this in the city. Of course, guys in the city play soccer in their free time but guys out here lift hay bales for fun and race tractors. I sigh as he tucks his shirt into the back of his jeans and walks out of sight.

"Tyler..." his name escapes from my lips before I realize what I'm saying.

"Savannah," I turn at the sound of my name to find a shirtless cowboy in the form of Tyler standing in my Aunt's kitchen. She snickers and scurries away. I swallow hard and try not to stare, but I can't help it. He grew up nicely.

"What are you doing here?" I already know the answer to my own question, but I need confirmation.

"I'm the ranch hand here."

My mouth drops open even though I had a feeling that was going to be his answer. He chuckles and shakes his head. This has to be whom my mom was so quietly talking about on the phone.

Chapter Five

Tyler

*M*y hand runs over my chest wiping away my sweat. I'm used to Aunt Sue seeing me like this – shirtless, sweaty and covered in dirt from working the ranch – but not women in barely-there clothing with their arms stationed at their sides and their lips pursed. Savannah swallows hard, making me wonder what's going through her pretty little head. Is she sorry that she had to move or is she plotting my demise for not recognizing her yesterday? I bet she's plotting my death. She sucks in her cheek in an effort to what – keep from smiling? Yeah, that's exactly what she's doing. Savannah looks at me and rolls her eyes. If I weren't still embarrassed about yesterday, I'd think her attempt to be prissy is cute. Hell, she is cute, but I can't be thinking about her like that. It's not right.

By most standards, not enough time has passed for either of us to forget each other. I know that people change over time and maybe she more than me, but her transformation from the waifish, mousy girl she was is unbelievable. And her toes... what is it with her toes that keep me staring? I've never been one to think feet are cute, but damn if her toes aren't painted pink against the tanned skin of her luscious, long legs, which are begging to be wrapped around my waist.

I chide myself for even thinking of Savannah like that. I don't care if our mommas had dreams that we'd be hitched; it's never gonna happen. Women like Savannah don't marry ranchers unless they're looking to get away from some crazy ass life in the city, and I know from Uncle Bob that's not the case here. Miss McGuire went and got herself into some trouble and has been sent back to God's country to repent, because around these parts we don't get in trouble. By looking at her, she probably broke a nail and needed rescuing by the local fire department.

I'm not hiding the fact that I'm checking her out and neither is she. I see her pink tongue dart out and wet her lips while I stand in front of her. Everything in me says to look away, to go on about my business and leave her be, but I'm a man and she's standing in front of me barely dressed - something her aunt and uncle aren't going to be too appreciative of. Hell, I'm appreciative, but I don't want to see her like this. I want her body to be left to my imagination.

"Put this on before your Uncle walks in here and drops dead of a heart attack." Aunt Sue throws a pile of clothes at Savannah causing her to jump. The clothes land on her head and slide down to the floor, as I stifle a laugh.

"It's not funny," she seethes as she steps into a pair of Aunt Sue's sweatpants. They're about ten sizes too big yet do nothing to curb the thoughts running through my mind about her long legs. She glares at me before sliding the sweatshirt over her head and yanking the hem down roughly. Even with the oversized clothes on, she's still gorgeous.

"Oh, I think it is." I have to turn away because I don't want her to see me smile. She's cute when she's angry and I don't need her seeing that she has a positive effect on me. I busy myself by grabbing a plate from the cabinet and pulling out all the fixin's to make my lunch. Aunt Sue provides the food. I provide the appetite.

"What are you doing?"

I turn my head over my shoulder and say, "I'm making my lunch. What does it look like?" Her expression is one of confusion. I don't get this chick at all. She murmurs my name and has no problem with staring at me, but when I'm standing in front of her, it's as if I'm a foreign object. Of course, I'm no better. I finally have her standing in front of me and I say nothing. I just stand there and let her stare. Most men would be okay with that, but I'm not. The past twenty-four hours have not gone the way I thought they would.

"Its breakfast time, isn't it?"

I look at my watch and shake my head, wondering what it would be like to sleep in until I could have a normal breakfast. "It is for people like you who don't get up before the sun."

"Can't you go home and eat?" Her tone is one that I'd expect from someone living in New York City, hell from any city for that matter, and just like that I'm pissed. I've been around long enough to know when I'm being talked down to. It happens all the time when the chicks come waltzing into Red's looking for action, thinking we're all dumb.

I chuckle lightly and mentally count off the days until she's out of here. If this is the kind of attitude I'm going to have to deal with when I come to work, I may need the damn summer off.

"I work here, eat my lunch here and if I have a hankerin' for some of Aunt Sue's supper, I'll stay for supper too."

"So you're always here?"

I turn around and lean up against the countertop with my ankles crossed. I take a bite of my sandwich and watch the frustration mask her beautiful face. "Ah, you askin' 'cause you're interested?" I waggle my eyebrows at her.

Savannah's eyes go wide as she crosses her arms over her chest, except she really doesn't have arms since she's swimming in her aunt's sweatshirt.

"Whoa, who's this?" Jeremiah has impeccable timing as always. If he had walked in a few minutes ago, he'd have seen her in a state of undress and would be looking for a way to get her out to the barn to ride his tractor. That's the last thing I want, him messing around with Savannah. He steps right up next to me with a piece of wheat hanging out of his mouth. He tips his hat toward her, only to be met with an icy glare.

"Well, if it ain't Mouse."

"Vanna," she says, icily.

I pat him on the back. "That's right, Mouse grew up when she started hanging out with the Yankees and now wants to be called 'Vanna'," I add, watching her face morph into anger.

"I don't care what this fine piece wants to be called, as long as the sound coming out of her mouth is my name."

I laugh and wish he was joking, but he's not. However, seeing the shock on her face as the words tumble out of his mouth are priceless, so I don't do anything to correct him.

"I didn't think you liked ice cubes that much, Jer."

"Oh, I'll make her warm."

"You're really disgusting," she seethes at us as she steps away. I can hear Sue in the other room trying to pretend she's busy, but her laughter is giving her away. "You'll stay far away from me or I'll tell my uncle that you're harassing me and you'll get fired."

"Doubt it," Jeremiah says as he winks at her. "Seriously, Mouse, what the heck happened to your braces and brown hair?"

She relaxes, dropping her arms to her sides. "What's wrong with you guys? You grew up. I grew up. You weren't all tall and... whatever." She moves her hands in an awkward motion toward us, solidifying my knowledge that she's been looking at me. The very thought makes me want to go pound out some push-ups or something so she has more to stare at.

"She wants us," Jeremiah says with a straight face, causing me to choke on my lunch. Savannah turns, throws up her middle finger and walks out of the room, leaving us standing there, each with our own thoughts. It's going to be a longer summer than I originally thought, especially knowing her and her big-city attitude are in full force.

Chapter Six

Savannah

I officially hate my life. No, hate isn't a strong enough word, but despise doesn't seem to drive home what I'm feeling right now.

Loathe?

Resent?

Revenge? Yes, that's what I want. Revenge. I want revenge on Tyler, Jeremiah and most importantly my mother. Not that I can come up with something clever or anything that would make a difference in my mom's world to show her how much I hate my life right now because of her.

I look down at the pile of manure and let my gaze wander to my boots. No, they're not even my boots, but my Aunt Sue's pink muck boots with stupid brown horses on them. Every part of me is sweating right down to my toes. I rest my head against the pitchfork, but only briefly before the smell of cow shit assaults my nasal passage. I'm going to need so much therapy after living here. I certainly hope that Paris has some amazing doctors with the capacity to brainwash away my memories.

I don't know how people wake-up here every day and act happy. There's nothing here. TV is questionable. No mall within a hundred miles. No Internet. No air conditioning. No cell service. I've literally stepped back in time and the highlight of my life is going to be the once a week trip I'm allowed to take into town — wherever that may be — to email my schoolwork. Lucky me!

"Savannah."

I roll my eyes, pick up the pitchfork and move the steaming pile of cow shit into the wheelbarrow. I know I'm the laughing stock of the ranch, but I don't care right now. Maybe in the back of my mind this was my plan all along — pack nothing but my summer wardrobe so they're forced to take me shopping. Anything I can do to get off the ranch and into civilization. So what if my uncle doesn't like my "daisy dukes" and crop tops? It's a hundred freaking degrees outside. He's lucky I'm not in my bikini right now.

"I called for you."

I stop and place my hand on my hip, cringing immediately at the thought of shit touching my skin. Dropping my hand, I look Tyler square in the eyes. Had he known who I was when he picked me up yesterday we could've hung out. But no, he had to be an ass of epic portions and ignore me. I thought for sure he'd at least be a little bit of a salvation for me while I was here.

"I'm here doing the work you said I had to do!" I wave my hand widely at the many piles that I'm supposed to move out to the "back forty," as he called it. After Tyler's early lunch, I was given my list of chores. At first I thought it was a joke. I couldn't believe my aunt and uncle expected someone like me to get dirty. Sadly, I was wrong, and I was ushered out the door. Even my cry about homework fell on deaf ears. I'm sure that comes later. I'm learning quickly that we use nature as a clock on the ranch.

"I see that. You've been out here for two hours and have yet to fill one barrow. You might want to pick it up because it's gotta get done, and it's either today or tomorrow."

"Whatever," I spit out as I dig the pitchfork into another overheating pile of crap. "What do you want, Tyler?"

"Well..."

I stop what I'm doing and immediately regret it. He's taken off his hat and is running his hand over the top of his freshly shaven head. When we were little I used to tease him about his curls, but he doesn't have them now and a part of me is wondering if they'll reappear if he grows out his hair. I suppose this heat doesn't mix well with longer hair. Lord knows I'm sweating something fierce. His blue eyes are a stark contrast against his tan skin, making them sparkle as if looking out over the ocean. His tan is real from working, not the fake type that the guys in the City often spend most of their time achieving under bulbs. I would know, since it was an every other day stop for me. On Tyler though, it's sexy, appealing and sadly the opportunities I have to see him shirtless no longer continue.

I look over his shoulder at Jeremiah who is taking out one of the horses. He's screaming something incomprehensible, which causes Tyler to look as well.

"Ignore him."

"I plan on it," I say automatically. It's dawned on me

that getting along with Tyler and Jeremiah will make my time here more manageable, but I'm not here to establish the connection we had when I used to live here. Those days are long gone and overtaken by superficial thoughts and selfishness. I'm here to do my penance and get the hell on a plane to Paris. I have a goal and I won't let some country boys ruin it for me.

"Can I get back to work, Boss?" Tyler blanches at my choice of words, which gives me very little satisfaction. I want to take back my words, but am afraid to show him that I care. He didn't care about me yesterday. Why should I show him my true feelings today?

"Actually, Aunt Sue has asked that I take you into town. She thinks you need some clothes suitable for working on the ranch."

I shake my head. "She just wants me to dress more like her."

"Don't know, don't care, Savannah. I have to go into town, she mentioned me taking you, said it might be nice if we stopped for supper. I'm leaving in fifteen minutes."

Tyler doesn't wait for me to respond. He turns and leaves me ankle deep in manure. I freeze when he takes off his shirt; watching the sun hit his back makes me ponder how different my life can be here if I let down my guard. Thing is, I did that once, and that's how I ended up back in his Podunk town. I bet Tyler knows I'm watching him as he bends down to pick up the hose. He turns on the water and splashes himself. The droplets glisten in the sun as they traverse down each ridge on his back making me wish I had a towel to offer. He doesn't exist where I'm from... and I can't exist here.

"Savannah?"

His voice breaks my daydream and I find him

standing in front of me. His chest is wet and drying quickly from the penetrating sun. My eyes travel down the front of his body. There isn't a patch of hair until his belly button and then... I force myself to look away.

"Why can't you call me Vanna?"

His lips pull into a thin line as he shakes his head. "Because that's not who you are to me, sweetheart."

Rolling my eyes, I rest my hip against the pitchfork. I look at him questioningly, fearful of what might come out of my mouth if I speak.

"I think you should go in and shower. Let me show you around."

"Is that so?"

He nods. "Jeremiah and I hang out at this place called Red's, you might like it."

"I'm underage in case you've forgotten."

"I haven't, but they don't care and no one is sayin' you have to drink. You can come or not, don't matter none to me. You have fifteen minutes."

This time he walks away and right into the barn, out of sight, but not out of mind. I don't know how I'm going to spend day after day working with him. He's my boss for the summer and there isn't a damn thing I can do about it.

Chapter Seven

Tyler

The radio plays one of my favorite songs and by favorite I mean one that I'll dance to at Red's. I think my back is permanently slouched from leaning over and looking out the window for Savannah. The clock on the dashboard tells me that I've sat in my truck ten minutes longer than I said I would. One quick look at the front door and I know she's not coming. If I were a betting man I'd say she went inside and asked her Aunt Sue about shopping. Sue would've likely played along for a few minutes, but Savannah's smart and she'd catch on. Her aunt didn't suggest shopping. I just wanted to get her away from the ranch so I could see if the girl I once knew was still inside. I just want to see her smile. She hasn't done that since she arrived, granted she's been here barely twenty-four hours, but still. A girl's gotta smile and from what I remember, Savannah has a killer one.

I drive away without looking back. The dust cloud behind me makes it impossible to stare at the house in my rear view mirror. I should be thankful that I can't see it. I'd probably throw the truck in reverse and go drag her out of the house kicking and screaming. Of course that means I'd have to put her over my shoulder and hold her legs down with my arm, which would undoubtedly come in contact with her ass and that would likely be my undoing. Yes, it's a very good thing I can't see the McGuire house right now.

Everything in my head is telling me to ignore her. To let her do her thing and not even bother making small talk. Uncle Bobby told me that she's off to Paris as soon as the summer's over, so getting attached only means heartache. Not that my heart beats for her or anything. But the thought of what Savannah was like when we were kids still lingers in the back of my mind. I know that Savannah is in there somewhere; she just needs to be let out. The girl I remember would've mounted any one of our mares for an early morning ride and would have told her uncle exactly what he can do with that chore list. Although, watching Savannah in those outlawed shorts and her aunt's muck boots was comical, I'd rather see her dress appropriately for working on the ranch. The last thing we need is for her to hurt herself or get some pesky bugs biting up her legs. Hell, maybe she needs to be taught how to live on a ranch. I suppose living in the concrete city, you forget what it's like to stop and smell the roses, or saddle up a horse and take a day trip out yonder. Maybe I'm just the guy to reacquaint her with life in the country, or maybe I just need to stay away from the enigma that is Savannah McGuire.

Coming to Red's was a bad idea. Inviting Savannah to come with me was even worse. At this rate, I'm destined to screw up something major and cause an epic catastrophe or go home with someone I shouldn't. That someone just walked into Red's and will surely be my breaking point tonight. Red's is packed and there ain't a place to park that won't make me walk a hundred yards to get in the door. When I spot Jeremiah's truck, I park in front of him, blocking him in. I figure I'll end up leaving before him anyway so it won't matter. I take one look in the mirror and give myself a pep talk. I can go in, have a beer, be cordial and go home alone. Or I can go in and let Annamae walk all over me, tell me how much she misses me and let her show me a good time in my truck. Either way, I'm screwed. I slide my hat on, adjust the rim and practice my best Tyler King 'resident cowboy' smile. Oh yeah, that's going to knock 'em dead.

The music is blaring and bodies are moving on the dance floor. The constant thunk of boots hitting the wood at the same time makes the floor vibrate. There are a few girls standing on the edge waiting for a two-step and some fella to come ask them to dance. They're all dressed similarly with their shorty shorts and cowboy boots on. I'm not usually a fan of this hoochie cowgirl style, except this is how I see Savannah dressing once she realizes she's meant to be on the ranch. These are the city girls that come down for the weekend, slumming it. They want themselves a real cowboy, but only on the weekends when their corporate daddies are off playing golf and not watching their darling debutantes. This is where Jeremiah thrives. Me? Not so much. Unless, of course, you're my ex and you're blocking my way into Red's.

I tip my hat to Annamae who has her hands firmly on her hips. "Evenin' Annamae. Haven't seen you at the honkytonk in some time, Rufus out of town?" I should be bitter, but I'm not. He saved me from a life of being a socialite's husband. Annamae would've never moved to the ranch and I definitely don't want to live where there's traffic.

"I've been tryin' to get up with you for days."

"Really? What for?" She hasn't left a message at my house so I know she's up to no good. It's just a matter of me figuring it out before it's too late.

"I hear you have a Yankee livin' with y'all."

Good news travels fast around these parts, except it's not news and Savannah's only been here for a day. "Yeah, where'd you hear that?"

Annamae shrugs. "Around."

"Uncle Bobby's kin, that's all."

"I don't know why you call him your uncle. He ain't."

"Blood isn't the only thing to make someone your kin, Annamae. Hell, we would've gotten hitched and you would've been my kinfolk." I shake my head at her. Her family is high cotton and all about status. No one is good enough for her family. "I gotta find Jeremiah."

Annamae looks over her shoulder and angles her head. I look around and spot him on the dance floor being sandwiched by two redheads. I don't know how he does it, but he's definitely smooth.

"Have a good night, Annamae." I leave her standing there to contemplate the meaning of life or whatever else she needs to think about.

"How do?" Della asks as she sets a beer on the bar for me. I nod in her direction, pick up my beer and spin to watch the line dancin'. Girls love it when a guy can dance, but I'm not into the synchronized dancing. Give me a two-step where I can hold my girl and let the music guide us and I'm happy. I can see Savannah and myself out there dancing. Hell, we used to dance on the porch all the time. She taught me how to two-step. I'm so much better at it now though, and I want to show her. I want to take her out there, place my hand on her neck and guide her around. I want to pull her close and let our bodies move in the same distinct motion. I want to feel her pressed against me and have my hat cover our faces when we kiss. These are all thoughts that I shouldn't be having about Savannah.

"Ah, well I'll be a monkey's uncle."

"What's wrong, sugah?" I turn at Della's voice and hang my head. "Don't go fallin' for the Yankee."

I look at her questioningly. "How'd you know about her?"

"Small town. Big bar. Everyone's talkin' about the hottie down at the ranch."

I look around the bar and shake my head. "Jeremiah gossips like a girl." Della starts laughing.

"Too right." She walks away, only to return with a full glass for me. "From what I hear, y'all knew each other when you were young'uns?"

"Yeah, she and her momma moved to New York City a few years back. Uncle Bobby says she got into some trouble and her momma shipped her back here to finish out school and for the summer. I don't know what she did and we ain't really talking yet, mostly on the count that I made a fool out of myself when I picked her up."

Della throws her towel over her shoulder and shakes her head. "Sweetie, I'm sure it wasn't that bad."

I spin around on the stool and cross my arms, resting them on the lip of the bar. "It was bad. I went and made this big ole scene, picked her up and swung her around, you know like you're always talkin' about in them books you read? Anyway, it wasn't her, just some random girl that got off the bus with her and ever since then, her demeanor is cold."

Della tries not to laugh, but can't hold back. I rest my head on my arm and sigh.

"Listen here, sugah, you have to remind her why y'all were friends to begin with."

"How?"

"Well I don't know Tyler, you have to find somethin' that was special and just go with it."

"You mean ask her out?"

Della shakes her head. "Not all girls want to go out. Just remind her of what a sweet, charming boy you are. She'll be putty in your hands." Della walks away to tend to the rest of the patrons, leaving me with thoughts of taking Savannah out on the horses or even four-wheeling. Thing is, I don't know if she likes those types of things anymore. If she were from here, it'd be a no-brainer and even though she is from here, she's changed.

Chapter Eight

Savannah

*E*very time Tyler walks by or his voice echoes over the ranch, images of him driving away with me standing on the porch continue to replay in my mind. They serve as a constant reminder that he and I are no longer friends. Being stood up is not high on my qualifying list of being friends. He is, according to Aunt Sue, my boss and I'm to do whatever he asks of me. I also have to complete his requests in a timely manner without any sass.

However, it's very hard to be near him right now. He promised me shopping and a stop at his hangout, only to leave me standing on the porch being swallowed by a giant dust cloud. The tears I fought quickly turned to frustration. Doesn't he understand that a woman needs more than fifteen minutes to get ready? I was standing knee-deep in manure for heaven sakes. I had to shower! He may be used to hanging out with women that smell like crap all day, but that's not me and it never will be.

To make matters worse, when he does walk by, he ignores me. Not that I want him to talk to me, because I don't. I have nothing to say... except I do, and it's not about taking me to town so I can submit my homework. I want to ask him why he stood me up. Why he made such a big deal about me going if he had no intentions of taking me. I had hoped after our brief conversation that maybe we were turning a corner and he and I would be friends, but it's clear that he thinks I'm nothing more than an employee to him.

I know I deserve this. I haven't exactly been approachable or worthy of any friendship. I don't want to be here mucking horse stalls or shoveling manure. This. Is. Not. Me. Life's unfair, I know that, but never in a million years did I expect my mother to decide she can no longer care for me because of my out of control ways. I get good grades and do what I'm told. Just because she found me in one compromising position doesn't make me a bad person. It makes me human. I know she's made mistakes in her life. Half the time she makes me feel like one.

When I boarded the bus to come here... a bus, not a plane... I told myself that a wall is going up and nothing will bring it down until I'm on a plane heading to Paris. My aunt and uncle may be the only family I have, but they don't know me and they definitely don't know my mother anymore. She's not the same person she was when we left here. Sometimes I wonder if moving to New York City was her downfall as well as mine. Frankly, I'm getting irritated hearing "remember when"... because no, I don't want to remember when I was young, carefree and had no worries in life.

Except I'm starting to and I'm afraid to ask any questions for fear they'll be happy and think I'm enjoying my time here. I'm not. If it's not the heat, it's the humidity and the smell. It's the looks I get when I come downstairs dressed in shorts or a dress. My aunt and uncle can't honestly say they've never seen a girl in a sundress before. I have eyes, I see the girls that show up to feed Jeremiah lunch. Their clothes are no skimpier than mine and lord knows what goes on in the barn when they get here. As soon as I hear the catcalls, I hightail it back to the house and hide in my room. It's the only safe place where I can escape. Tyler can't bother me there and watching him eat lunch in my aunt's kitchen really bugs me.

I fill the horses' water trough and replace the hose where Tyler likes it. I'm done for the day and now have to find the courage to ask Tyler if he can drive me into town. I know it's something my uncle discussed with him before I got here, but I have to make the arrangements. Uncle Bobby says that Tyler's in charge on the ranch, I do what he says and Tyler will be accommodating. We both know the latter is not true.

I kick off my unfashionable pink boots and leave them by the back door. My toes wiggle from the freedom they're feeling at the moment. I know I'm missing the essential clothing necessary to survive on a ranch. I was hoping to take care of that minor issue last week when Tyler offered to take me shopping. Little did I know he was just kidding with that invitation.

He's leaning up against the counter when I enter the kitchen. The non-benefit of having a big ole country house is that when the screen door slams, it alerts everyone in the house that someone's coming. Maybe that was my intention, because I definitely could've snuck up on him and if I had done that, he wouldn't be facing me right now, eyeing me up and down like he has done every day since I arrived. I'm not sure if he's expecting some-thing with me to change or not, but if he is, he'll be waiting an awfully long time. I'm me. He can take it or leave it. Part of me wants him to take it, but I'm not willing to admit that out loud. I've done enough pining over high society boys, and the rejection that they dish out is enough to last someone a lifetime. To them, it doesn't matter what your mother does now, it's whose blood runs through your veins. Regardless of her checkbook balance and club memberships, I'm still an outsider to them.

It took me a year of speech therapy to drop my Texan accent. Being teased one too many times about saying "fixin'" or "y'all" had me visiting five days a week until I could speak without a southern drawl. I was still an outsider, but they were my friends. Tyler used to be my friend and so did Jeremiah. The memories of the three of us running in the fields, climbing hay bales and swimming in the pond are slowly starting to come back. I can try to fight them, pretend they don't exist and just live my life as this outsider on a ranch not really fitting in anywhere, or I can start exploring on my own.

I walk right up next to Tyler, my hip brushing him out of the way. My elbow bumps into his back as I maneuver to make my lunch. I don't need to be in here, but it's where I want to be. I feel his gaze on me, but refuse to acknowledge him. He's breathing loudly... either that, or we're just close enough that I can hear him clearly. Every-thing in me is screaming for me to turn and glare at him, but I don't. I just continue to make my lunch and allow my arm to touch the back of his shirt every chance I get. If he wants to be a jerk, fine. I'm going to be a tease.

Tyler clears his throat and adjusts his legs, crossing one over the other. I'd like to think that I'm getting to him, but the reality of the situation is that I'm probably getting on his nerves. One final elbow to his back, followed by a shallow groan and I'm moving away.

"Did ya have to elbow me?"

I turn and set down my sandwich. I mimic his stance with my ankles crossed and my hands resting on the countertop behind me. I tilt my head slightly, open my mouth just barely and say, "Huh."

"Huh? Is that how they taught you to articulate yourself in that fancy private school in New York?" His words bite.

"What do you know about my school?" I bite back.

He shakes his head, pursing his lips. "Nothin'," he replies, walking out of the kitchen.

I shake my head at his retreating backside and turn away. "Oh my god, he's so frustrating," I mutter under my breath.

"I'm frustratin'?" he roars. I turn in time for him to step right into my personal space, his face inches away from mine. His finger is pointing at me and his lips are moving but nothing is coming out of his mouth. He bites down on his lip and says, "I'm not frustratin', Savannah. You are."

Okay so now we're in first grade and we're going to do the – 'you are, not me' game. No thanks. That game I do remember and hated it.

"How am I frustrating? I didn't invite you out and then stand you up," I challenge as I step toward him, forcing him to take a step back. "I didn't promise shopping and a little bit of freedom only to drive away leaving a dust bowl in my wake."

"I waited for you. You never came out. I told you fifteen minutes."

I scoff. "Seriously, Tyler, I'm a girl, I need more than fifteen minutes to get ready. I don't know what type of girls you like, but I, for one, would like to not smell like crap when I'm going out. It's hot outside, I was sweating and you had me shoveling poop all day."

He covers his mouth and steps away from me laughing. I punch him in shoulder and turn away, only for him to grab me by my waist, holding me in place. My skin warms where his palm is resting on my hip. An unknown sensation courses through my body making me feel nervous. I didn't feel like this when... I shake my head, trying not to think about what happened in New York. Chalk it up to a bad experience with the wrong guy and what not.

"You're laughing at me. I don't need or want to be here right now," I say to break the tension in the air.

"I'm sorry, Savannah. I'm only laughin' because you said poop and I think it's cute. In fact, I thought for sure you'd start cussin' up a storm by now, but I haven't heard a single one come out of your mouth. I'm sorry about the other day. I waited, I did, but when you didn't come out I figured you weren't comin' and I bailed. I got pissed and took off, lettin' my temper get the best of me."

I turn slowly, noticing that his hand hasn't moved yet and is still firmly holding onto my hip. "I stood on the porch and watched you drive away." I know I sound whiney, but when we were kids, that's all it took for Tyler to make sure I had my way.

His fingers dig into my hip as if he's trying to hold on. "I'll make it up to you," he whispers as he steps closer. His fingers relax and I feel them move over my skin ever so lightly. I look at him for some type of sign that he wants to be my friend and am taken by the small smile that forms.

It's not the same one he gives to my aunt Sue when he sees her. This one is different. It's mine. His hand disappears the moment the screen door slams, but it's too late. Jeremiah is snickering in the doorway and pointing. I step away, putting space between Tyler and me.

"We headin' to Red's or what?"

I look at the clock and wonder why he's going to the bar now.

"Yeah," Tyler replies as I feel myself sag with disappointment. "First, I have to take Savannah shoppin'. I promised her last week. I'll meet you there." I smile, but still feel let down. I'm not good enough for this Red's place, clearly.

"Don't forget the condom."

I blanch at Jeremiah's retreating backside. Tyler is looking at the doorway he occupied not seconds earlier. I see his face turn blazing red. He turns back to face me, but keeps his eyes focused on the ground.

"Ignore him. I'll wait while you shower."

Tyler doesn't give me an opportunity to respond. He's walking away muttering something under his breath that I can't understand. I jump when the screen door slams and he yells for Jeremiah. I step over to the window just in time to see Tyler tackle him and they get lost behind the fence and tall grass. It's funny to see two grown men play fighting. For the first time since arriving, I'm smiling because I'm happy; even if I have a feeling it will be short-lived.

Chapter Nine

Tyler

"You're such an idiot, Jer. I swear you were dropped on your head as a kid!" I kick him in the ass as I move away from him. He's such a little punk sometimes, saying that crap in the kitchen. The last thing I need is for Savannah to think I'm into her, or that I'm looking for a quickie. I'm going to deny any feelings I have for her until I'm blue in the face, especially to Jeremiah. That boy is the town gossip. I want Savannah to feel comfortable around me and if that means I have to hide how I'm feeling and pretend that I'm just trying to get my friend back, or get to know the person my friend has become, then so be it. I don't need Jeremiah making a fool out of me in the love department. I can do that just fine on my own.

"Man, you're ornery." Jeremiah stands and brushes off the imaginary dirt and grass from his shirt and pants. "I reckon you have an itch that you're about to scratch."

I lunge at him, only for him to sidestep and laugh. I'm breathing heavily out of frustration, my chest puffing in and out. I'm going to kick his ass. He pulls off his hat, twists it a few times and takes a bow before walking away from me.

"You need to learn to keep your yapper shut," I yell at his backside. He doesn't stop, but raises his arm and flips me off. Stupid asshole. "She's our friend," I say, for both my benefit and his.

I take off my ball cap and run my hand over my face. I'm afraid to look at the house because I have a feeling she's watching this whole thing go down. If she is, maybe I'll be lucky and she'll just think that we're two stupid morons who like to wrestle in the grass. I glance at the window, and sure enough, she's standing there. I can't see her face clearly, but she notices me staring and moves away quickly. Hopefully she's going to go shower or do whatever she needs to do so we can head into town.

I'm mentally taking a note of the kind of clothing she needs to survive out here. She may not want to "Countrify" her wardrobe, but I'd feel better if she was adequately protecting herself when she's out here working. Her uncle put me in charge of her chores and the day-to-day lack of proper apparel puts limitations on what I can have her do. Not to mention her aunt's boots are too big for her and she looks like she's wearing clodhoppers, which she is too dainty for.

"Ugh," I chastise myself for even thinking of Savannah as dainty. Since when do I have thoughts like that? I shake my head in an attempt to clear them. Except, I'm failing miserably. It's not because I don't want to, but she's making it impossible with the barely-there sundress she now has on. She stands not far from me, one long, perfect leg drawing all my attention as she taps it impatiently. Oversized sunglasses, the same ones she was wearing when she got off the bus, shield her eyes, making it impossible for me to see her expression. Her lips are pursed and painted. A large red bag hangs from her shoulder, the same type Annamae carries and I can't help but wonder if Savannah has her "life" in there. I know I should look away but I can't. My eyes follow the path of her long, tanned leg until it reaches the hem of her dress. Without much control I swallow hard and adjust myself discreetly. I close my eyes and berate myself for allowing Savannah to turn me on.

I move toward her and her posture immediately changes. For the love of all things holy, I want to rip those sunglasses off her face so I can see her expression, so I can read her. I hate not being able to see what her eyes are trying to tell me.

"Are you going to change?" her tone is snotty and just like that she's back to being the bitch she's been since her arrival. I want to know what happened to the girl that was in the kitchen with me not so many minutes ago and why the ice queen is back.

I clear my throat. "Yeah, at my house," I answer as I walk away from her. Just like day one, she can follow or not, but either way I'm done with her hot-and-cold attitude. I don't really give a flying shit if she wants to come to town with me. I can't continue to put myself out there if she's going to act like a Class A bitch all the time.

Surprisingly, she follows in line behind me. I pause briefly when we get to my truck and contemplate whether or not I should open her door. After some debating, I decide against it. It's not that I'm not a gentleman, but she has no respect for me. Here I'm willing to take her to town, and she has attitude. Girl seriously needs to be put on a bull and have that shit bucked out of her.

She seems to have no qualms about opening her own door and we both hop in at the same time. As chivalry dictates, I could shut the sliding window behind us, but I think I'll wait until the princess asks nicely. Besides, maybe the wind will blow sweet nothings into her ear and she'll come out of the funk she's in.

We drive approximately three hundred yards before I park. Savannah raises her sunglasses, resting them on top of her head. She looks out the window and then at me, her face full of confusion.

"I thought we were going to your house?"

I chuckle. "This is my house." I hop out of the truck and walk to my front door. The soft smell of pine greets me. I breathe in deeply and admire my freshly installed floors. When Jeremiah told me about the lumberyard getting their hands on some wide-planks, I couldn't resist. It took me three weeks to get the floor down and polished, but it was worth it. My house is small, but it's mine for as long as I want it. The two bedrooms are large and accommodating, but with only one bathroom it can be a little cramped when my mom comes to visit. Last summer I installed a bay window, but haven't done much else. This winter I plan to replace the mantle and maybe update the kitchen. Aunt Sue did a lot of work before I moved in, but it looks more like a cabin than a home. I turn back to see her sitting there, looking straight ahead. Leaving the front door open, I give her a choice of whether or not she wants to come in, but I'm really not counting on her doing so. I head right to the shower so I don't keep her waiting. The sooner we're out of here, the better. After tonight I won't have to take her shopping again.

Letting the hot water beat down on my back relieves some of the stress I'm feeling. I can't let her get to me. She's changed so much since she's been gone that it's unfair of me to expect her to be the same, or to adapt to our laid back way of living. The country and city just don't mix that well. Thoughts of her sitting in my truck, with beads of sweat forming on her forehead because of the sun plague my mind. I slam the water off and get out. I don't want her bitching about me taking too long in the shower and the fact that I even care what she thinks pisses me right the hell off.

Opening the bathroom door, I step into the living room, cinching my towel tightly around my waist. My dumb ass didn't think about bringing clothes into the bathroom with me when I left the front door wide open, and it should have because Savannah is standing in front of me, her crystal blue eyes roaming up and down my body. If I weren't happy with the way I look, I'd wonder if she was impressed. I've worked hard on my physique, keeping myself in shape. I could wink as I walk by, but she's standing in my way. I can either return to the bathroom or stand here like a wanton piece of art and let her gawk. I encourage her to get her fill of me. I want to be ingrained into her memory so that when she's far from here and she looks at another guy, she only has flashes of me. I want her to see that I've also grown up and that neither of us are those two kids that everyone remembers.

Maybe that's what I want. Maybe in the back of my perverse mind this is what I need – for her to see me, like this, in my home. What purpose that serves, I have no idea, other than getting us both flustered. The thought of touching her skin, like I did only an hour ago in the kitchen, forces me to step back. I'm not crossing the boundaries she's put up. She quickly licks her lips, her wet, pink, tongue showing briefly before she pulls it back into her mouth. The urge to kiss her is there, but if I do, I'll lose my towel and neither of us is ready for that to happen.

Savannah sways ever so lightly from foot to foot. Her demeanor has changed from when we were in the yard. This is the Savannah that I want to know, not the icy cold bitch from earlier. If I can have this girl, I'd start spending every free minute with her.

"What happened to your house?"

I clear my throat and rub my free hand on my towel. "It burnt down about a year after you left. Mom and I moved closer to town, but I didn't like it. I missed the ranch too much. When I turned eighteen, Aunt Sue showed me this place. She had been restoring it for a while and was going to rent it out, but figured that I didn't much like staying in your pink bedroom. I moved in and started working for your uncle. As soon as I graduated, I went full-time and started taking some classes online, which sucked because I had to do it at the library, but it all worked out. After I finished my degree, Bobby handed over a lot of responsibilities. I can afford to move now, but I like this house. It has everything I need." I look around, afraid to make eye contact with her. She asked me a simple question and for some reason my mouth went on a verbal tangent.

"You lost everything?"

"I did," my answer is barely a whisper. I don't know if she realizes it, but there's so much meaning behind her choice of words and the fact that she said "everything". I felt lost when she left. I know it wasn't her fault, but I couldn't help but be mad at her. She left me. She was my best friend, and she moved away. Losing my personal belongings was just the icing on the cake during an already depressing year.

"I'm sorry."

"For what? You didn't set my house on fire."

She shakes her head and steps closer... too close. "No, I didn't, but I can still feel bad that you lost everything."

I should step back and put some distance between us, but I can't. I don't want to. "I lost my most important possession earlier than that. It wasn't harmed in the fire."

Her eyes meet mine and I can see the realization in her blue orbs. "Me," she whispers. I nod, unable to deny her this answer. She steps forward, the fabric of her dress brushing against my towel. Her fingers dance along my skin, causing goosebumps that I haven't felt in a very long time to pebble my skin. The trail she leaves ignites something in me. Many images flash before my eyes, all of them ending up with me sans my towel and between her legs.

"Savannah," I murmur, huskily. She responds by allowing her fingers to trace my jaw.

"I didn't want to leave," she admits quietly.

I nod, unable to hold back. I slip my arm around her waist and pull her closer. Her chest, heaving as her breathing picks up, brushes against mine. She's a smart girl. She knows what's coming next. "If you don't want me to kiss you, please step back. I won't be mad."

Savannah bites her lower lip, tilting her head to the side. Her hand moves to my head and her fingers running over what little hair I have left. I don't hesitate as I move forward and press my lips to hers. Immediate warmth mixed with chills takes over my body, and I try to pull her closer while keeping my hand securely fastened to my towel. One false move and she's going to see how much this kiss really means to me.

Chapter Ten

Savannah

*M*y body trembles. My heart thumps wildly against my chest. Tyler's arm holds me securely to him while my fingers play with the short hairs on his head. I wish his hair were longer so I could run my fingers through it and feel the silky strands as they caress my fingers. I understand why he keeps it short, but for once I want this fantasy to play out – the one playing out in my head where he drops the towel and carries me off to his bedroom while I thread my fingers through his locks, pulling as he climaxes. Not that the scenes running through my mind as I anticipate his next move aren't making me hypersensitive to his actions.

His eyes dart between my mouth and my eyes, the dark orbs of his pupils hijacking the vibrant green I've become accustomed to as they widen. I don't know what they're conveying, but I hope he's seeing that I want him to kiss me, that I need him to kiss me. I know I don't deserve his attention, let alone his affection, but I want it.

I've wanted it since he walked into the kitchen and told me who he was. The feelings I had when I left, the ones my mother told me were wrong and that I was too young for, are rushing back with each and every moment. As much as I want to deny they exist, I can't. As much as I want to keep my wall up and pretend like he doesn't matter, he does. He was my best friend and now he's standing in front of me, hopefully about to kiss me.

I can feel the rise and fall of his chest. Our breathing matches, keeping us connected. My eyes flutter as his lips touch mine. They're soft, softer than I thought they would be. They still against mine, as if he's cautious, waiting for me to pull away and start running for the hills. I didn't know it until he touched me like this, but I've been waiting for this moment my whole life. I want more. No, I need more. I have to know if he's feeling the same crazy mixed up nervousness that I am when he's around. I need to know if his palms sweat when I stand near him, because mine do. Does his heart pound so hard that he fears if he doesn't walk away people will hear? If I could tell him... if I could find the words or find a way to show him that I want him, maybe everything would be okay.

The kiss is too quick, and he pulls away. At best he gave me a peck. That's all I'm worth to him. It's all I deserve. I let my hands fall in defeat. He catches one, placing it over his left pec. I swallow hard as my fingers caress his skin. I feel his skin pebble under my touch and knowing that I'm doing that to him turns me on. I don't know why he's hesitating because right now I think he knows what I want.

My eyes meet his. They're gleaming. He turns his head slightly before placing his hand on the back of my neck. He wets his lips and moves toward me painstakingly slow. I try to move closer, but I'm sealed to the ground. He smiles, sensing my need. I've never felt an urge quite like this. If he doesn't kiss me soon, I'm going to kiss him whether he likes it or not.

The anticipation is too much to bear, so I don't wait. I take control. I grab the back of his head and pull him closer to me, closing the inches enough for him to know what I want. I briefly catch a smile before my lips take his. If this is what he wanted, and I caved, I lose. Right now I don't care because I feel his tongue move against mine masterfully. He steps back, righting himself along the wall, spreading his legs just enough for me to step between them. I feel his towel brush against my leg and then skin, lots of skin.

My hand roams over his chest feeling the definition of his muscles. My fingers work to memorize each ridge and valley. I reluctantly remove my hand from his hair and to his back. He shifts away from the wall, allowing me easier access to touch him. He presses himself against me, letting me feel what I'm doing to him. I whimper as he pulls me closer with both of his hands on the side of my head. He's no longer holding the towel and I don't even care. Having him kiss me like he's wanted this is all that's important to me and all of a sudden I'm lost in everything Tyler.

Tyler pulls away, breathing heavily. Our breathing is in sync as if we're one. He peppers me with kisses along my eyes, cheeks and finally the corners of my mouth before placing his lips on mine again, albeit briefly before he pulls away.

"Sweet baby Jesus, Savannah that was..."

"Perfect," I interject. It was for me and I can only hope that I've met his expectations. My hands drop from his body, both screaming with desire to touch him again. I clench my fists tightly, afraid that I might be overstepping or feeling something he's not.

"Perfect would be an understatement. You don't know how long I've waited to do that." My body sighs happily that he feels the same way and I try not to smile. He rests his head against the wall and gazes at me as his fingers trail down my arm before linking with mine. If I move my eyes, or step away slightly I know I'll be seeing all of Tyler. I'm not sure how much control I'd be able to maintain so I keep my eyes focused on his and try to read his expression.

"Come here," he murmurs, placing his hand on my cheek. "For as long as I can remember, I've had dreams about kissin' you and those dreams hold nothin' on reality. I know you have a lot going on and if this ain't right for you, don't be afraid to tell me. I'm not going anywhere."

I pull my bottom lip into between my teeth and nod. "I had this vision of what it'd be like when I got off the bus, ya know? I thought I'd come down the stairs, and you'd be waiting. I'd jump into your arms and everything would be the way it was when I left."

"Except I screwed that up because you look nothin' like the Savannah that left me five years ago."

"Is that bad?" I ask with a bit of fear in my voice. The last thing I want is for him to not like me because I grew up.

He shakes his head. "Hell no, it doesn't matter what you look like as long as you don't mind being in my arms. We need to get to know each other and believe me when I say this; I plan to get to know you all over again. You've been gone for a long time and we really haven't been gettin' along but that can all change." He swallows as his thumb moves back and forth on my cheek, gently caressing it. "You're so beautiful and as much as I want to continue standing here, I'm naked and unless you plan to take care of my issue, I'd like for you to turn around so I can grab my towel. As soon as I'm dressed I can take you on that shoppin' trip I promised."

I hesitate because honestly there's nothing stopping me. He raises his eyebrow, calling me out on my stalling tactic. I give him the eye roll that I know pisses him off as I turn around. I hear him shuffle behind me and when his arm comes around my waist, I don't think twice. I lean against him and am rewarded with small kisses on my neck.

"You have no idea, Savannah," he says against my skin before walking away. He's right, I don't, but I really want to find out.

I barely have time to register that he's gone before he's standing in front of me again, this time in a dark t-shirt with his sleeves rolled up over his biceps. His shirt is tucked into dark blue jeans and of course, he's wearing his cowboy boots. For the first time since I've been here, my idea of what my ideal man would dress like has changed. He's not some city guy with a rich family. The image now is of a man who's wholesome and hardworking, everything that my friends back home would scoff at. Thing is, I like what I'm seeing, even though I'm leaving at the end of the summer.

"Ready?" he holds out his arm for me, adding to the already growing list of things I like about Tyler.

"I have to stop at the library to send my homework."

He looks down at his watch and sighs. "We'll have to drive fast," he laughs. Somehow I think that's not a problem for him.

He walks us out of the house and shuts the door behind him, never letting go of my arm. When he walks around to the other side of the truck, I realize that this is the first time anyone is going to open the door for me. It's crazy how this simple gesture makes my heart beat faster.

"Thank you," I say as he holds my hand, helping me into the truck. I'm not shy about staring at him as he runs around the front and hops in. I'm trying not to smile, but I can't help it. Earlier today, when I was waiting for him, I was pissed. I thought he and Jeremiah were badmouthing me. It was my typical girl bullshit, always assuming the worst. I need to learn that not everyone in my life is out to get me or hurt me.

"After you do a little shoppin', we'll stop for supper and then I want to take to you to Red's and introduce you to Della."

The instant he says a female's name, my body tenses. Maybe Tyler's no different than the guys back in New York. Maybe he's just better at hiding it than they are. I stiffen when he reaches for my hand, but I let him hold it just to save face.

"What's wrong?"

How he knows something's wrong is beyond me. "I'm fine." I attempt to convince him but my smile is stilted and I turn to look out the window.

My hand clenches his as he barrels off the side of the road, digging up gravel and dust. Before I know it, he has my seat belt undone and I'm almost sitting on his lap. His hands cup my face, forcing me to look at him.

"I'm not playing games, sweetheart. That kiss back there? I meant it. Now tell me what just soured your mood."

"Who's Della?"

"Ah honey, she's the bartender, and she's heard all about you probably from Jeremiah and his big girly mouth. I just wanted you to meet her, that's all. I'm not one who goes around kissin' beautiful girls when I have someone else to keep my bed warm at night. The moment I heard you were comin' back," he stops and shakes his head. I don't know if he doesn't want to tell me, but I want to know. "I'm fixin' to say some seriously girly shit and if you laugh I'm going to take you over my knee, ya hear me?"

I nod and stifle a giggle. Sometimes, Tyler's southern drawl is heavy and other times he acts like he's not some straight-up southern cowboy.

"When Uncle Bobby mentioned you were comin' back, I thought this was a chance for us to see if we really had a connection the way I remembered all those years ago. I made sure I had no loose ends before you arrived."

"Loose ends, as in girls? Do you have a girlfriend?"

"No ma'am." His smile is so wide and his eyes are gleaming. "Unless you want to be."

I roll my eyes. "Ah shucks, Billy Bob, when you go and ask me like that, how can a girl resist?"

Tyler chuckles and leans in for a kiss. "I'm going to have so much fun with you tonight." He brushes his lips quickly against mine and nudges me back to my seat. "Yee-haw," he screams loudly as he steps down on the gas pedal, his tires spinning up dirt and gravel as the tail end of his truck shakes back and forth. This is the Tyler King I've been waiting to see.

Chapter Eleven

Tyler

*T*oday is moving entirely too slow for my liking. Each time I look at my watch, only a minute or two has passed and I know my work is suffering. I'm not sick or hung over, just infatuated, and I took the menial task of moving hay bales into the horse barn so I could be close to Savannah. She's cleaning the horse stalls today, a job that I gave her so I could stare at her. So I could see her smile at me each time I pass by... and with each smile, my steps falter a little bit more, but it's worth it.

Last night was more than I ever expected. When I came out of the shower and saw her standing there waiting for me, my breath caught. The sun was beaming through the front window, shining on her just perfectly. She was glowing as if she were an angel, even though I knew she was far from it. Her piss pour attitude from earlier still weighed heavily on my mind. But she surprised me. She moved closer. She touched me. That moment was everything I had hoped for and never thought would ever happen.

Yesterday I did things I never thought I would enjoy. I shopped, carried bag after bag and I held her hand proudly. There were stolen kisses under the awnings of storefronts and heated ones against the side of my truck. By the end of the evening, Savannah had stocked up on everything she needed to make it through the summer, including a pair of cowboy boots. I tried to buy her a hat, but she wasn't having it. The plan was to take her to Red's, but when we arrived, they were closed so they could resurface the dance floor.

I hated leaving her at her front door and driving to my house. When I looked toward the big house, I could still see her silhouette standing on the porch. All I could think was that she was watching me, maybe waiting for me to come back. If she wasn't Savannah, I would've. I would've kept her out all night and not cared about work the next morning or what her family might think. But this is Savannah and I work for her uncle. Bobby and Sue are my family and I respect them. I won't be doing anything to mess that up.

I lift another bale of hay and set it on top of the stack. My t-shirt is soaked with sweat and I think today's a perfect day for a dip in the pond. I glance over my shoulder at Savannah who's dressed like a country bumpkin in overalls, tank top, muck boots and a ball cap. Her hair is braided and in pigtails. Annamae used to do that, and I hated it, but on Savannah, it looks freaking sexy as hell.

"What ya staring at, cowboy?"

My eyebrow rises slowly as I bite back a smirk. "Cowboy, huh?" I'm not gonna lie, her giving me a nickname does something to me. I make a mental note not to tell Jeremiah that I like it because he'd just tell me I've turned into a sissy and ask if I need to change my tampon.

Savannah shrugs and my eyes immediately fall to her bare shoulder. It's beckoning for my lips. Many times throughout today I've wanted to take her into one of the stalls – a clean one of course – and have my way with her. I know just having her pressed against my body for a few minutes would be enough to curb my desires. No, I'm lying. A few minutes would be torture.

"I kind of like it. It fits you."

I tilt my head and smile, confirming that yes I do like it, but some things are better left a secret. Making sure the hay bale is secure, I walk over to her. I'm trying to strut, to be sexy, but I'm not sure if I'm succeeding. I've never put much effort into impressing a girl before, but with Savannah it's different. She's used to high-class rich guys and I'm just a country boy with not a lot to offer. I'll never drive some sporty car that costs more than my house, or belong to some ritzy country club. There'll be no vacationing in the Hamptons for me. I'm okay with this lifestyle. I'm also not stupid enough to think that Savannah's willing to give all that up to make a home with me here.

As the brief glimpse of a possible life with Savannah flashes through my mind, I pause mid-step and quickly divert my eyes to the now fascinating concrete floor that she hosed down not twenty minutes ago. I don't know where the thought of her making a home with me came from and as much as I can see a future with her, I know that's not what she sees. I'm not a stupid man, a hopeless romantic maybe, but definitely not stupid. She's too young, and she has dreams of her own. I know she's leaving and nothing I do or say will stop her. I won't even try. She needs to live out her dreams. But Paris, France is light years away from Rivers Crossing, Texas and I know she'll forget all about us back here. It's what I expect.

"Ty-ler," her voice sings out, reminding me that we're still in the present day and not months away from now. She's standing there in her stall leaning up against her pitchfork, watching me. I know I can play this two ways: I can go over and kiss her good and proper or I can pull her pigtails like I used to back when we were running amuck and walk out. Neither will protect my heart and the reality of the situation is that she already owns it. If anyone would've told me when Savannah McGuire walked out of my life five years ago that she'd return and have me thinking about sharing a home, I would've punched them in the face.

I never thought my momma was in her right mind when she told me that Savannah and I were going to get hitched someday. I used to yell at her for teasing me. If she could see me now, standing here like a fumbling fool, she'd kick my rear end all the way to town.

"Cowboy?" her voice is full of desire as she purrs my new nickname. That's my undoing. I move as if a donkey has kicked me in the ass until I'm standing in front of her. Taking the pitchfork from her, I set it outside the stall and shut the gate. The only parts of us that are visible are our heads and shoulders.

"What d'ya say, wanna roll in the hay?" I know my joke is corny, but I'm going for results.

Savannah pulls her lower lip into her mouth, a sure sign that she's thinking too hard and looks out the barn door. Her smile is mischievous and daring. I pick her up and she laughs, wrapping her legs around my waist. Lowering us onto the fresh hay, I set myself on her gently.

I lean in for a kiss and let my lips linger on hers until I feel her hands press against my back. This situation has bad news written all over it, but I'm not thinking with my head right now.

I pull away and smile down on her. "What are ya doin' tonight?"

She shakes her head. "I'm pretty much a homebody right now."

I mentally kick my own ass for asking such a stupid question. Of course she's not going anywhere. Bobby and Sue hardly go out and I know I'm her transportation.

"Jeremiah's havin' a bonfire at his place. Wanna go?"

"That sounds like fun. Will there be a lot of people?"

I nod. "He doesn't do small. I usually crash at his house because he gets a keg, but I don't have to. We can throw a few blankets in the truck and watch the stars later if you want."

Savannah runs her hands up my t-shirt and I try not to cringe with embarrassment. It's soiled and I'm sweating. The last thing I want is for her to get grossed out by me. I start to lift off of her, only to be pulled back.

"Leaving me so soon?"

She doesn't know the meaning behind her words. I'll never leave, not her and not this ranch. This is my home and my life. I shake my head and feel my lips go into a tight line. I could say so much right now and have no doubt that most of it would scare her away. Hell, my thoughts are scaring me and I have three years on her.

"I'm dirty," I admit to her, staying with the safest answer to her open-ended question.

"I don't care, Tyler."

"What changed?" It's a question that's been sitting on the tip of my tongue since last night. Savannah did this complete turnaround and while I'm grateful, I'm also skeptical.

Moving to the side, I leave half my body still on her. She moves her leg, locking it behind mine and effectively keeping me in place.

"Yesterday when I went inside to get ready, my mom called and I thought she'd be happy to talk to me, but she wasn't. She was short and rude, reminding me that I screwed up and that I better not do the same crap here too. I was so angry that I took it out on you. You were trying to be nice, and I didn't deserve it. When you left me in your truck, I thought, 'Wow, I must not be important to him either.' I went into your house thinking I'd snoop. Treat you like you were treating me, but when I saw the pictures of us on your mantel, something inside of me clicked. I started remembering us before I moved and how I used to smile. How you used to make me smile. My friends in New York, they don't smile, not like you and Jeremiah."

"How do we smile?"

Savannah moves so she can see me clearly. "When you smile, you light up the whole room. Your smile means that you're happy. I haven't smiled like that in years and wanted to remember what it felt like."

"So you thought you'd kiss me?" I ask, playfully.

"No, that was something I wanted to do since that day in the kitchen. I just didn't know how you'd react. I mean, I had a pretty good idea from earlier in the day when you held onto my hip, but I was being an epic bitch and was just praying you wouldn't push me away."

"I'd never push you away, Savannah."

She snuggles into my chest, draping her arm around

me. I'm not sure if this is the right time, but I have to ask. "Sweetheart, why'd you get sent here?"

She sighs and moves her hand to the back of my head. Her fingers glide along the nape of my neck. "I had a party. Mom was never home, I was lonely and desperate to fit in. You know at first when we moved, things were great. We went to the park, toured some museums, all stuff we didn't do here, but she quickly got promoted and started spending more and more time at work or when she was home, she was locked in her office. My mom was rising up the ranks as one of those big time celebrity lawyers you see on TV and while she looked great and powerful to everyone else, she was ignoring me. I could go two, three nights before I'd see her and one night I reached my breaking point. I invited friends over and things got out of hand. She um... caught me with a boy in my bed. I was drunk and there were people all over the apartment in various states of undress. She found some cocaine residue on her mirror and freaked out. Even though I passed the drug test she gave me, she still opted to send me here to fix myself."

I pull her closer, hugging her to me. Life here is so laid back, but I get that her mom would be mad. "I'd be pissed too if I came home and found you like that."

"Pissed enough to send me away, or to start coming home from work at night?"

She had me there. My mom was always home by dinnertime and is always there when I need her. I didn't grow up not seeing her. "My anger would be more directed at the boy in your bed. That would piss me off the most, but work is never more important than family."

"It is when you're trying to screw the boss's niece. Get the hell up you lazy asses."

We both jump, causing Jeremiah to cackle loudly as he leaves the barn.

"Shit," I mutter. "I didn't want him to see us."

Savannah pulls away quickly, scrambling to her feet. "Why not?" there's pain in her voice. I reach for her, only for her to pull away.

"Because he's an ass, that's why. He's a freaking child, Savannah. It's not because I don't want him to know, it's because of the torment we're going to receive. Believe me, sweetheart, I'll be shouting that you're mine from the rooftops when we decide to make it official."

"What's it going to take?"

I pull her to me, capturing her lips with mine. "You tell me."

I leave her standing there with her mouth wide open. It'd be so simple to just fall into her life and be with her if she weren't leaving. I can't be the one to make a decision on where we're going. If she wants to have fun, I'll show her a good time. If she wants to be together, I'll be there willing and waiting for her to break my heart in the end.

Chapter Twelve

Savannah

I rush through my homework, knowing that Aunt Sue won't let me go out with Tyler tonight if it's not done. It doesn't matter that it's Friday; rules are rules here, and they're not meant to be broken. I know they mean well, but it's hard to concentrate knowing that Tyler is waiting for me. He's going to take me on a date. Well, I'm calling it a date. I don't care that it's not to some five-star restaurant with a maître d' and fake accent. It's a night with Tyler and his friends and I want to see him interact, see who he's become. I want to learn what makes him tick and how to make him laugh. I have a feeling he's different in front of his friends. I just hope he doesn't put up a front while I'm there.

My mind drifts back to the barn and how comfortable I was in his arms. My heart was racing, laying there with him on top of me. It wasn't like before, when my mom caught me. Everything about that night was wrong. The way he touched me. The way his lips felt against my skin.

I had expectations and feelings that I thought would surface, but they never did. With Tyler, my senses are heightened. I don't have to wonder how my body will react because it knows him. How it can remember him from when I was twelve is unbelievable. I know our moms used to joke that we'd get married when we were older, but I never thought anything of it. Poppycock is what Uncle Bobby would say, but maybe they were right. What else explains my sweaty palms, my inability to breathe and the anxiousness I feel when he's around? It's not just when he's standing next to me but when he's across the pasture or standing in the kitchen. I feel his presence all the time.

I should be scared because, when you think about it, it's creepy having those types of reactions when you hardly know someone. My knees shouldn't go weak when he smiles at me. I shouldn't find myself smiling at the silliest of thoughts, things like when he brushes up against me, but that's what I'm doing. I can hear my heartbeat over the loud roar of the tractor and not just when he's near – it's in anticipation of when I'll see him. I didn't know how today would go. I wasn't sure if I'd see him before lunch. He made sure I did, working alongside of me until it was quitting time. For the first time since I arrived, I actually loved my job today.

My cursor blinks at me, reminding me that I should be filling the screen with useless words that don't mean anything to me. Homeschooling has a lot of benefits, one being if I ace this paper I'm done with this class. Sure I'm going to miss graduation in a few weeks, but I don't care. When my mom busted the party, they all went running. Not a single one of them stayed to help clean up, or helped me to diffuse the situation. Not a single one of them spoke to me the following Monday at school, shunning me due to their own selfish reasons. They left me alone, throwing me to the sharks of high school rejection.

The more I think about it, the happier I am that my mom sent me here. In just a few weeks I've remembered what it's like to live here, breathe the cleaner air and relish in the calm that comes with living out in the country. I miss the amenities that living in the city provides, but I'm managing. It's nice not to be tied to my phone all the time, or sitting in my room surfing the web.

I look out the large picture window that faces the driveway, the same driveway that will lead to Tyler's house if I were to walk that way. I'm tempted to get up and start the trek, just to see what he's doing, maybe even pretend I was just out for a leisurely stroll. He'd know I'm fooling, but that wouldn't matter, not in my eyes.

I let out a heavy and dramatic sigh only to hear Aunt Sue giggle from the kitchen. I should talk to her, confide in her. I know she won't tell my mom how I'm feeling or what I'm doing, but she might tell Uncle Bobby and I don't want him freaking out on Tyler. Uncle Bobby doesn't need to know that Tyler was in a state of undress with me pressed up against his body alone in his house. I don't want Tyler to get into trouble for my actions. It wouldn't be fair.

Aunt Sue appears with a tall glass of sweet tea and a plate of cookies. She sets them down in front of me and pulls out the chair to my right. When she sits, she sighs in a more dramatic fashion than I did a few moments earlier.

I laugh and shake my head before taking a sip of her homemade brew. Uncle Bobby says it's the best I'm ever going to taste. I'll have to take his word for it. None of my friends would be caught with ice in their tea.

"What's on your mind, sugah?"

"Me? I'm not the one who exhaled a year's worth of breath when I sat down!" I wink at her, letting her know that yes, I'm in a good mood and she won't get any sass from me.

"Well, there's something I want to talk to you about."

"What is it?" I ask, shutting the screen on my laptop. Out of respect, I'm giving her my undivided attention. Not that the black vertical line blinking at me is going to get any of it.

"I know I'm not your momma and I never pretend to be, but you're here in our house, livin' under our roof and we have rules that you're expected to follow."

I'm slightly confused by what she means. I've done everything she and Uncle Bobby have asked of me and I've done my chores without too much complaining. I know I'm a pain and didn't want to be here, but I've adjusted.

"Did I do something wrong, Aunt Sue?" I change the inflection of my voice and throw in the "Aunt Sue" to help diffuse whatever situation is brewing.

"Well, not so much, but I just want to have a woman-to-woman talk. Ya see, Jeremiah was flappin' his yapper again and said somethin' about you and Tyler... well you were..." she starts wringing her hands and I can only imagine what Jeremiah came in here and said. It makes me wonder if Tyler knows how much of a busy body that boy is. Maybe Jeremiah and I need to have a sit down about his gossiping.

"Just spit it out so I can tell you the truth."

"Well, gosh darn it, Jeremiah said you and Tyler were humpin' in the hay."

If my mouth had been full of sweet tea it would now

be all over the table. As it is, I find it hard to form a sentence to counter what she just said. I look away, not because I'm ashamed, but to gain a tiny bit of composure. I have to give Aunt Sue credit. At least she's not yelling like my mom or throwing breakables at my head.

Folding my hands in front of me, I square my shoulders before answering. "Aunt Sue, Tyler and I weren't humpin' in the hay. We were lying there, talking."

"Is that boy takin' liberties?"

"No!" I shake my head adamantly. "I like Tyler... a lot. But we weren't doing anything wrong out there."

Aunt Sue leans forward and places the palm of her hand against my forehead. I look at her like she's crazy, but she continues to flip her hand over before doing the same on my cheeks. "Are you sick?"

"What? No," I answer quickly, moving away from her hand. "Why do you ask?"

"Because not so long ago you stood in my kitchen throwing daggers at the boy with your eyes and shortly after that, you were stompin' around muttering his name with so much malice that I thought you were going to darn near kill him for something. What's going on?"

I can't help smiling and wishing that things were different when I got here. Being forced to do something against your will makes you hard and bitter and I took that out on everyone here. No one deserved it, except for maybe Jeremiah, but still. I was rude and know I have to change things fast before I ruin too much.

"I woke up, Aunt Sue. It was the sun, the air and the birds chirping. Heck it might even be Sundance because every time I go to clean her stall, she gives me a kiss. It was Tyler, being selfless and accommodating to my attitude. It was my mom, reminding me that I'm trouble and that she's still angry, yet you and Uncle Bobby aren't treating me like that."

I take a deep breath and smile. "I don't want to be angry all the time. I know what I did was wrong, and I apologized, but my mom won't listen. I'm only here for a few months and should try to make the best of it. Am I excited for Paris? Yes, I am, but that doesn't mean I need to make my life miserable while I'm here."

"Well I'll be darned. You went and fell in love with Tyler, just like your momma said you would."

My mouth drops ever so slowly. Only to be lifted back into place by her soft fingertips. "It's okay, sugah, we've just been waiting for this day to come."

I shake my head. "Aunt Sue, I'm not in love with Tyler. Sure, I like him, but love... I don't even know what that is. I'm too young to be in love and Tyler... he's definitely not in love with me."

"Well whatever you young'uns are, you need to be careful. Don't go lettin' Bobby catch you with your pants down."

"Aunt Sue, Tyler and I were fully clothed. Jeremiah is just being a gossip that's all."

She nods but the expression on her face tells a different story. She thinks we're having sex, and that thought horrifies me. I don't want her thinking things like that. As soon as she's busying herself in the kitchen, I high tail it out the front door. The guys are still working and I know Uncle Bobby has gone to auction, so he's not going to see this.

Jeremiah is driving the tractor, mowing down the hay so it can settle for the next few days before they turn it into bales. Standing in his path, I make sure I give him plenty of time to stop what he's doing. Once the engine stops, he stands and tips his hat.

I march over to him and beckon him down with my finger and a sweet smile, which seems to do the trick, because before I know it's he's climbing down with a shit-eating grin on his face.

"What's up, darlin'? You lookin' for someone better than ole Tyler?"

I close my eyes and imagine the scene playing out in front of me. My hand forms into a fist and before I know it, my arm is back and moving forward at a break neck speed, connecting with his chin.

"What the – "

"Oh, holy mother of – "

"What the hell is going on?"

Jeremiah, Tyler and I are all yelling. Jeremiah is holding his chin. I'm holding my hand against my chest, trying not to cry. Tyler is running toward us at full speed. This is not how things played out in my head.

"Savannah, what the hell?"

I look at Tyler with tears in my eyes and see nothing but confusion all over his face. "Tyler, he went and told Aunt Sue that you and I were humping in the damn stall."

"You what?" he roars at Jeremiah who is still holding his face. He doesn't seem to care because he's not agreeing or disagreeing, he's just standing there.

"What?" he shrugs. "I was just sayin'."

"Dammit all to hell, Jeremiah, her uncle is going to kick my ass."

Jeremiah spits and thankfully there's no blood. Tyler moves over to me and pulls my hand away from my chest.

He rotates my hand back and forth and wiggles my fingers.

"Doesn't look broken," he mutters. "Jer, sometimes I think you're out to get me killed."

"Nah, man, just laid."

I start to say something but he's climbed back onto the tractor and turns it on. He wouldn't be able to hear me if I yelled. Tyler shakes his head, takes my hand in his and walks us to the house. I'm learning really quickly that Jeremiah says what's on his mind whether it's correct or not.

Chapter Thirteen

Tyler

We walk back into the house. I have one hand on Savannah's back and the other cradling her injured hand. I know what Jeremiah's doing; it's what he always does, creating a comedic yet drama-filled situation to gloss over his own insecurities. My only guess is he has a crush on Savannah, which I really can't fathom because he knows how eager I was for her to get here. Yes, my feelings have changed these past few weeks, but he knows that I'm definitely into her.

"I can't believe you hit him," my voice is soft, caring. Savannah leans into me, her head brushing lightly against my nose. I breathe in deeply, taking in the coconut shampoo she uses. She smells like summer and warmth. She makes my days brighter just by walking into my line of sight.

"Well, I can't believe he said we were doing it."

I chuckle lightly. It's nice to see the slight subtle changes in her. When she got here, she was hardcore and mean. Nothing was going to penetrate her tough façade, but I did. It took some time, but it was done.

"Would it be so bad if we were?" I close my eyes and wait for her to stiffen in my arms. I can't believe I let my mouth get the best of me. She has to know that guys, especially me, think about her like that. She has a rocking body, and the thought has crossed my mind a few times.

"Sorry," I shake my head. I know it's a dumb question to ask. Hell we aren't even a couple. We've just been kissin'. I haven't taken her out on a date yet and taking her to Jeremiah's tonight doesn't really count. There will be a lot of people hanging around and it's probably the least romantic thing I could do for her. Tomorrow I'm going to have to take her out, wine and dine her, and show her how special I think she is.

Savannah stops one step below me. She holds her hand out in front of her while I push her hair over her shoulder. She looks up at me and without hesitation I lean down and kiss her. I'm trying to make up for putting my foot in my mouth. I don't want her thinking that I'm only hanging out with her to get into her pants, especially after what she told me earlier. I had a feeling that her being here had something to do with another guy. Deep down I didn't want to know, but she's told me and I'm not going to use that to my advantage.

"I'm not saying it's bad, Tyler. What I'm saying is that Jeremiah telling my Aunt is not a good thing. She wanted to have the 'talk' with me, which was slightly awkward and when she used the word humpin', I swear I turned fifteen shades of red. You should've been there."

I lean my head to the side and laugh. "Oh, sweetheart, I would've loved to be there when this all happened." Shaking my head, I look into her blue eyes. "I'm sorry

Jeremiah is such a dink. He'll never learn and it doesn't matter how many times I beat his ass. Although, since you just cold-cocked him, maybe that's his lesson. If you don't want to go there tonight, we can do something else."

"No, I want to go."

"Okay." I look around quickly to see if there are any prying eyes before I lean down again and kiss her. Her lips are sweet, soft and taste like candy. They're reminding me of our make-out session – one that I want to revisit, repeatedly. "Come on, Rocky, let's get you some ice." I take her hand in mine and lead her right to the kitchen where Aunt Sue gasps as soon as we walk in.

"Sweet baby Jesus, what did you do?" she takes Savannah's hand in hers and directs her to the sink where she promptly puts it under cold water. "You need to wash off the germs."

Savannah looks over her shoulder at me, her eyes questioning her aunt. I shrug, not having a clue what she's talking about. Sue McGuire is what the town folk call "old country". She grew up in a house full of women who cooked, cleaned and had their own home remedies for every ailment and injury. By all accounts, you'd think Aunt Sue was some grandma type just milling around the house, but that's not the case; she can't be a day over forty.

"What in the blue hell is going on in here?" Uncle Bobby comes stomping into the kitchen and sets his lunch pail on the counter. He immediately kisses Sue before looking from me to Savannah.

"Sugah, what'd you do to your hand?"

"I punched Jeremiah, Uncle Bobby."

"Well, now why'd you go and do something like that?"

Savannah looks from him to me and back at him. She pulls her lower lip into her mouth and I see the tension in her jaw. I'm not going to let her get into trouble because I can't keep my hands and lips to myself.

"Because –" I start to answer before I'm interrupted.

"Because I'm an ass, Bobby, you know that. I was pullin' on her pigtails and makin' fun of her boots," Jeremiah saunters over to Savannah and stands between her and Bobby. "Girl's got a mean right hook, I'm tellin' ya. Look at my busted up lip, Bobby." He moves right in front of Bobby so he can see his face.

"Y'all need to be workin' and not flirtin'," he mutters as he walks out of the room with Jeremiah hot on his tail. I breathe a sigh of relief. Sue finishes wrapping Savannah's hand in a towel packed with ice and as soon as she leaves the kitchen, I'm moving to Savannah's side. My hand grazes her hip sending this dynamic sensation up my arm and right into my chest.

"He just saved us," she says, stepping closer. I'm getting the feeling that she likes living on the edge. I'm not sure how her Uncle will take it once he finds out we're messing around.

"Yeah, he did." My voice is quiet and Savannah takes that as a hint to give my lips and mouth some attention. My hands cup her face, holding her to me so I can relish in this brief intimacy we're sharing. "I think we should go," she whispers against my lips.

We don't have to be at Jeremiah's until later, so the fact that she wants to be alone with me excites me. I nod, pulling her hand into mine and walk us to the front door. We stop briefly to say goodbye and are shooed away by Bobby and Sue. We both shrug, but take it as a sign that they don't care that we're leaving together, although, Bobby probably thinks I'm just taking her to town to turn in her homework or shop. He doesn't know about the thoughts going through my mind when it comes to his niece. If he did, he'd take me out to pasture and shoot my ass.

It almost makes me feel bad, until I look at her and realize that getting shot would be worth it.

We spend a few hours just driving the back roads, Savannah sitting next to me with my arm resting on her shoulder, until we pull into Jeremiah's. Without a doubt, he invited everyone he knows and then some. The faint sound of music can be heard, the laughter is present and the flames of his massive bonfire are visible from the front of his house.

Savannah squeezes my thigh, letting me know she's ready to go. I bring her hand to my lips, gently kissing her bruised knuckles before we leave my truck. She reaches into the back and pulls out the blankets I set back there for tonight.

"Want me to carry those?" I ask, reaching out.

"I got it," she replies before kissing me quickly. It hits me right then and there, like a ton of bricks, that I'm screwed. This girl – the one I was trying to ignore – has already burrowed her way into my life whether I was ready for it or not. Who knew that something so simple as carrying blankets would be the trigger? We walk hand in hand to the backyard where Jeremiah has the most epic bonfire setup. Last summer we cut down logs and placed them in a circle. We also filled our trucks with sand and put that on the ground to give his area a beach feel. He said the chicks would dig it and they do, which is evident by the male-to-female ratio here tonight.

I introduce Savannah to the guys while Jeremiah boasts about his fat-lip, the tale changing each and every time. I'm going to have to tell him how much I appreciate him not saying exactly how he got it. I don't want any of these guys to get the wrong impression of Savannah.

We scope out a spot to sit and I help her spread out the blanket. I don't remember doing any of this stuff with Annamae. She used to do it all herself and never complained. Maybe that's why she cheated.

Before I sit down, I take Savannah's hand in mine and ask her if she wants a beer. I'm making an assumption that she's had one before. I never thought to ask if she drinks.

"Yeah, I'll take one."

She holds my hand until our arms are extended and just our fingertips are hanging on. "Hey, Tyler?"

I stop and stare at her. The way she says my name makes my heart beat faster. I move forward so we're chest to chest. "Savannah," I say huskily as I slip my fingers between hers.

"What happens if neither one of us can drive home?"

I smile and look around, checking out the night sky. "I have a feeling with you next to me, the bed of my truck would be pretty damn comfortable." She looks at me with a fit of fear in her eyes and I know I have to remedy the situation quickly. "I'll only have a few, I promise." I kiss the tip of her nose and wink at her before walking toward the keg.

"Hey Smalls, what're you doing in town?" I pat an old classmate on the back while he fills his red solo cup.

"Not much, King. But it's Dan now. I'm trying to grow out of that teen boy stage."

I look at him all cock-eyed. "Right, what's new?"

He moves aside so I can fill my and Savannah's cups. Looking over my shoulder, I spot her talking to Annamae – this won't be good. I regret chatting up Smalls because now I have to at least pretend to listen.

"I'm engaged. We're getting married in August."

"Wow, man, congrats. Does she know you're a two pump and dump chump?"

"Screw you man, I was fifteen when that happened."

"Still a great story," I laugh, shaking my head and tipping my cup back. "See ya later."

"Hey, is that your girl?" he calls out behind me.

"Yeah she is," I reply over my shoulder with a big ass grin on my face.

Bracing myself for what I'm about to walk into, I make my way back to where Annamae is still talking Savannah. I don't know what she's telling her and I don't want to know. Either way, if I have to spend the rest of the night reassuring Savannah that Annamae doesn't mean anything to me, I will. I just pray that Annamae ain't filling her head with a bunch of nonsense. Our time is short as is and I want a drama-free summer with this girl by my side.

Chapter Fourteen

Savannah

*W*atching Tyler is quickly becoming a favorite habit of mine. That is, until my vision is blocked by Dolly Parton. I look up and smile at the girl in front of me. She's country through and through. Or at least what I'd consider country. I know I bought cowboy boots, but I drew the line at the hat. If I'm going to wear one, I'm taking it off my own cowboy.

"You must be the Savannah I keep hearin' so much about?" Her hands are on her hips with her hip jutting out so that her leg extends to the side. Her toe taps and I'm not sure if it's to the music or if she's trying to assert herself somehow. For all I know, she's Jeremiah's girlfriend.

My brows furrow at her tone. "That's me," I answer plainly.

"I'm Annamae. I'm sure you've heard all about me." I shake her hand out of curiosity. I'm not here to make enemies and really don't want Jeremiah pissed off at me.

As is, he's sporting a shiner because of me. But the fact is I have no idea who she is.

"Nice to meet you," I put forth. It wouldn't be so bad to make friends while I'm here, even if soon I'll be in the City of Lights, sitting in little cafés and sipping on a cappuccino. Looking over her shoulder, I see Tyler heading back to me and can't help the smile that's building the closer he gets. I can see a gleam in his eye when he makes eye contact with me.

My lips part as he hands me one of the red cups. Tyler places his arm on my shoulders as he pulls me closer to him. Our lips meet automatically, both of us knowing that we needed to connect, even if it's just for a moment. I can't explain it and I'm not sure I even want to, but I have this never-ending tingle whenever he's near and it only intensifies when he touches me. I never want it to stop, but know the end is near. I'm going to have to figure out a way to have him and Paris in my life and I'm not exactly sure how I'm going to manage either.

"Ahem!"

Tyler sort of pulls me partially behind him, as if he's shielding me from something evil. I place my hand on his chest while my cup filled with beer rests near his hip. He tips his head to Annamae in a friendly gesture.

She steps forward, too close for my liking. I look at Tyler, who shakes his head ever so slightly. He lifts his cup to his mouth and takes a long drink. The sight of his Adam's apple moving mesmerizes me for some reason.

"So y'all together?"

I look up at Tyler and wink. He smiles and kisses me briefly, yet another habit that I'm starting to really enjoy. I could really get used to the type of treatment.

"I see you've met Annamae?"

"Did you tell her about me, Tyler?" she asks. I'm not even able to answer his question before she butts in. Apparently her presence in his life is important, at least to her.

"I'm sorry, he didn't," I shake my head slowly, trying to suppress a smile. Clearly, she feels as if she's an important part of Tyler's life and he doesn't because he hasn't mentioned her. Yet, she felt the need to come over and make her presence known. Shame I don't feel it's needed.

Annamae huffs and glares at Tyler. I want to slink back and hide from her daggers, but I stand firm. Clearly she's someone in his life.

"I'm his fiancée," she all but yells. My arms stiffen and I drop my hand from his waist. He quickly clamps his hand down on mine, holding it to his chest. Before I can say anything, he's speaking.

"Ex, Annamae, and we were never engaged. You made the decision that I wasn't good enough for you and shacked up with the landscaper. I don't know what you're tryin' to pull here, but it ain't gonna work. Savannah doesn't need to listen to your lies. Go find Rufus, he'll entertain ya."

My mouth drops open slightly and Tyler just shakes his head. He motions for us to sit down and I take the lead, pulling his hand into mine. He sits down first and pats the spot between his legs, which I gladly take. I lean back, settling in his arms. My body sighs when he drapes his arm over me. When I look back at Annamae, she's in the arms of another man... Rufus, maybe? Either way, it doesn't matter. I'm all too aware of women causing drama when it's not needed.

"I'm sorry about Annamae."

"No need to be sorry," I reply.

"We dated for a year until she met Rufus. Things didn't end well."

"Breakups never do," I mutter. I wouldn't know. While I've kissed plenty, I never made it to that "stage" where I could call someone my boyfriend. "Just Friends" is the title that has been used in the past. That was until now. I have no doubt I could introduce Tyler as my boyfriend and he'd agree.

Tyler rests his head on top of mine. "She's harmless, but you'll see her a lot. She likes to think that what we had was something great. Truth is, I probably would've married her had we stayed together and honestly I'm thankful that we didn't. She's really stuck up and way into her social status."

"Sounds like girls from my school, all for show and very pretentious. But this is nice. It's my first time at a bonfire and everything seems so free here... nothing seems fake," I mumble the last part. The more time I spend here, the more I realize just how fake I was in New York. I was trying to be someone I wasn't.

"The country will do that for you," he whispers against my neck. I turn my neck slightly to give him better access. As soon as his lips touch me, I shiver.

"Are you cold?" he asks as his hands start rubbing up and down my arms. I'm anything but cold.

"Not at all," I say loud enough for him to hear as I snuggle into his neck. Right now I wish we were some-place else where we could be alone. With so many prying eyes I don't want people staring at us. I turn back around and watch the others. Jeremiah waves and I hold my cup up, acknowledging him. I probably shouldn't have hit him, but I was angry. I suppose I need to learn to take everything with a grain of salt. In hindsight, he probably only deserved the punch if he had told my Uncle Bobby that Tyler and I were humping in the hay.

Tyler and I sit by the fire, listening to all the surrounding conversations. I'm content, being in his arms like this and don't want to leave. He holds me as if it's our last night together and not our first. I don't even want to think of what our last night will be, assuming of course we're still friends. With my track record I'm likely to screw this up before the weekend's over and I'll be back to square one, tiptoeing around him and being on the receiving end of his "I'm the boss" attitude.

We get up and walk around some of the property that Jeremiah lives on. His parents own it, but only use it for horses, not farming or anything like my Uncle Bobby. Tyler tells me Jeremiah works for him because his parents aren't running a ranch and that's what he went to school for. It's hard to believe my Uncle Bobby makes enough off his ranch to have employees. Tyler says the ranch thrives and does well.

It's not something I'd want to do, live on a ranch and work. I have goals, dreams. I plan to major in fashion while in Paris. I want to live in a flat above the busiest street so I can hear the traffic at night and be able to listen to the street performers. I want to live close to the park and watch the tourists stare at their surroundings in awe. I'm going to have this in a few short months and I can't wait.

Everyone comes over to talk to Tyler and he introduces me to all of his friends. At one point during the night I overhear him say that I'm his girl. I try to hide the cheesy grin in my face, but I'm pretty sure he sees it. Thing is, he doesn't turn away or try to hide that he said it. He keeps glancing at me while talking to his friends.

He makes me feel like I matter.

After the party dies down, I carry the blankets back to the truck and climb in as Tyler holds the door for me. He wants to take me stargazing tonight. My hand rests on his thigh, his arm around my shoulder as he drives down a dirt road. It's a good thing he knows his way around because I'd never be able to find my way home with all these roads that stretch on for miles and seem to lead to nowhere.

He pulls over in a field and kisses me on the cheek. "Wait here." He turns the truck off and everything is pitch black. If he thinks that I'm going to get out now, he has another think coming. I startle when the back of the truck starts to move. My heart is pounding so hard it feels like it's about to burst out of my chest.

The truck door swings open and I scream. "What's wrong, sweetheart?"

"Nothing, you just scared me."

Tyler reaches for my hand and helps me out of the truck. I clutch onto the sides of his flannel shirt and follow, bumping into him a few times before we reach the back of the truck. He lifts me onto the tailgate and jumps up next to me.

"Wanna lie down?"

"Yeah," I reply as I scoot back. Tyler's made us a bed back here, complete with pillows. I lie next to him and watch the sky. "Oh my, what was that?"

"Lightning bug. Don't you remember when we were little, and I caught one and put it in my mouth. My cheeks lit up. It looked like I had a light switch in my mouth. My mom was yellin' about me being taken over by aliens."

I laugh and remember the night he's talking about. We were so young, and he was teasing me about being a baby because he was older. I cried to my mom, and she told me I'd get my revenge when he became my husband. At that time, I thought Tyler had cooties and didn't want him touching me – especially if he was putting bugs in his mouth.

"I should catch one now."

"Oh, hell no," I say quickly. "If you do that, I'm not kissing you."

In the darkness I feel him adjust. His arm comes around me as he moves closer. "I'd much rather kiss you than stick a bug in my mouth."

"That's good to know because bugs are gross, but so are boys."

"Good thing I'm a man," he says before his lips crash down on mine. This kiss is different from the others we've shared. While it starts out slow, I can feel the urgency in the way he's holding me. His tongue caresses mine in a slow, languid motion. His lips mold to mine, making us one. Hands roam- his, mine, ours together.

My hand slips under his shirt and the need to feel him against my skin is prevalent. I wiggle until we're touching, only for him to sit up and remove his shirt. It's too dark for me to see him so I have to rely on my hands to tell my mind what I'm feeling.

His muscles are toned but not bulging. They're perfect. He hisses when my fingers graze his nipples. I smile, knowing I've elicited that response from him. I hook my finger into his belt loop and pull him on top of me. He doesn't hesitate as he settles between my legs.

Tyler moves against me, denim on denim creating enough friction to cause me to squirm. My fingers dig into his back, urging him to keep going. His lips are needy and move from my mouth to my neck and back.

"Savannah, we have to stop." Not the words I want to hear, but he's right. We're out in the middle of nowhere and as much as my body thinks I want this, I'm not sure if I do. Tyler shifts off of me but just barely. He kisses my neck lightly, small yet intimate gestures. "I don't want you to think that I don't want to go there with you. I do, but not out here and not until we've had a proper date. I'm havin' a hard time keepin' my hands to myself, I'm sure you've noticed, but I want to do right by you. I want to take you out and show you that I can be the gentleman you deserve."

"I've never had anyone say something like that to me before."

Tyler moves up to rest on his elbow. "You're so freakin' beautiful and I'm one lucky bastard to have you in my arms. All the guys tonight, they wanted your number and all I could do was laugh at them because you were goin' home with me. I'm gonna take you out tomorrow, just you and me."

"As long as I'm with you, Tyler, no one else exists. You can take me to the carnival for all I care. I just want you by my side."

As soon as the words leave my mouth I know I've just bought myself a whole lot of heartache.

Chapter Fifteen

Tyler

With one last look in the mirror, I run my hands down the front of my white button down and make sure it's tucked into my Wranglers. My sleeves are rolled up and my black Stetson is on. I'm ready for my first of what will hopefully be many dates with Savannah. I need to make the most of her days here on the ranch. I don't want her to forget me when she's off "decorating" Paris. The thought of asking her to stay a little longer has crossed my mind, but it's not fair of me to ask. She needs to see that she belongs here, that this is her home. I can't force her to see what I'm seeing if she's not ready.

Last night, I almost took it too far. She was there, urging me, but taking her like that – our first time – is not how I pictured us finally connecting. I'm not trying to be some poor romantic, but dammit if the girl doesn't deserve something better than a pick-up truck fuck.

I take one last look around my bedroom. I tidied up

last night after I dropped her off, dusted and vacuumed – two chores that I never think about doing. I made my bed this morning, thinking that my mom would be proud of me if she were here right now. I'm hoping to take Savannah to see my mom. I know she'd like to see Savannah, but I'm sure the feeling that she lost her best friend will surface again. It took my mom a long time to get over the total break in communication that took place when they left for New York. We were all hurt.

The flowers that I bought earlier this morning are sitting by the door, waiting for me to take them to Savannah. I never brought Annamae flowers; maybe that was where I went wrong. Either way, I don't want to mess up with Savannah. I close my eyes and lean my head against the door. I need my mind to stop thinking that she and I have a future after this summer. She's leaving. I'm staying. Paris is no place for a guy like me. I'd be lost unless we're out in the country with a few horses and a cow or two. But that's not what Savannah wants. I heard her talking to some of the girls last night – she wants Paris for its culture, fashion and cobblestone streets. She's excited to sit in the little cafés and sip fancy coffee with her pinky finger in the air. None of that appeals to me. If anything, I need to reeducate Savannah McGuire on why her place is here.

I know I need to show her everything that she can have here. There's the pond, the horses and the long nights under the cover of stars. And there's me. She can't have this in Paris. Tonight after dinner, I'm going to take her out to the pond on horseback to remind her that she once loved it here and never wanted to leave. If that doesn't work, I'll need to convince myself that I can let her go when the time comes. After only a few weeks of her being here, I'm in deep and don't know if I can survive her leaving me again.

The drive over is short and doesn't really afford me the opportunity to settle my nerves. I need to shut off my mind and stop thinking about what will happen at the end of the summer. Even though the situation feels out of my control, I need to do everything I can to try and change her mind.

As soon as I slam the door to my truck, the front porch door is shutting as well. With each step I take, she's taking one. When I reach the bottom step she stands before me, six stairs away, staring down at me. I swallow hard as I appraise the sheer beauty before me. Her long blonde hair is curled with half of it pulled up, accentuating her neck. Thin straps are all that cover her shoulders, making my mouth water with thoughts of how much freedom my lips will have. Savannah's dress is white, stopping at her knees and perfect against her tan skin. But what does me in are the brown boots that she's wearing. She's the most gorgeous cowgirl I've ever seen, even if I can't get her to wear a hat. With her standing before me like this, it solidifies my belief that she belongs here.

Savannah's gaze falls to the flowers hanging by my side. I look down and smirk. I can't believe I forgot about them. "Um..." I clear my throat, ridding myself of the imaginary frog playing around with my voice. I don't know what this means, but standing here in front of her makes me nervous. "These are for you." I hold out the bouquet of sunflowers. The florist in town said I should go for roses, but Savannah doesn't look like the "roses" type. She's more sunshine and happy.

"They're beautiful." Her steps are painstakingly slow as she walks down each stair to me. With her standing one step above, she's almost my height and my instinct is to wrap my arms around her and carry her to my truck. It dawns on me right there that a night in town at a restaurant where people can see us just won't work for me. I want to be alone with her, surrounded by what's brought us together.

"Can you wait right here for a minute?" I thrust the flowers at her, causing her to startle slightly. "Shit, sorry," I mumble as I climb the stairs two at a time. As soon as I get to the door, I turn to see Savannah admiring her flowers and I can't help smiling.

Rushing into the house and right into the kitchen I find Aunt Sue taking an apple pie out of the oven. It's hotter than blazes outside and she's in here baking, God bless her.

"It smells delicious, Aunt Sue," I say, inhaling the smell of apples and cinnamon. I'm surprised Uncle Bobby doesn't weigh three hundred pounds with all the baking she does. I know I would if I ate here every day.

"It's on the table," she tells me without looking in my direction. My brows furrow in confusion as I look at the table and find exactly what I'm looking for.

"How'd you know I wanted the picnic basket?"

She stops and turns. "I saw her gettin' dressed and you aren't a boy who likes fancy restaurants. It's all in there." I walk over to the basket and lift the lid to find fried chicken, green beans and cornbread. Surprisingly, there's a bottle of wine even though we're still underage. The fact that she's okay with it shows me that she's okay with me pursuing her niece.

My head shakes slightly. "I'm going to take her over to the pond. I think she'll like it better than going to some stuffy restaurant." Picking up the basket, I head to the back door. "Thank you." Aunt Sue nods and moves on to her next pie, leaving me with too many thoughts running through my mind.

I hustle to the barn and saddle Sundance. She has a fondness for Savannah and won't mind if we ride tandem. I have to transfer the basket that Aunt Sue put together into some saddlebags. Not ideal, but there's no way I can strap a picnic basket down to the saddle. I pull a blanket out of the tack room and make sure it's secure before leaving the barn. I'm sure I've forgotten something, but I'll improvise.

Leading the horse around the front, I find Savannah sitting on the steps, twirling her flowers around. Honestly, I'm surprised to find her still sitting there, but she's waiting for me just like I asked.

"Hey, sweetheart." She looks up and her mouth drops open. "So I had this big fancy dinner planned in town, but that's not me." I shrug, hoping that she's okay with this. "Truth is, I don't know what type of date guy I am, but horseback riding out into the sunset seems like a pretty good time to me." I look over my shoulder before looking back at her. "I have supper here and thought we could ride out to the pond."

I pull my hat off and run my hand over my hair. "I think I have everything for a –" Savannah is in front of me before I can finish my sentence and places her fingers over my lips.

"It sounds perfect," she tells me with a smile. When she removes her fingers, I take advantage of the moment and kiss her.

"I'm really nervous," I add for good measure so she doesn't think I'm a fumbling idiot.

"Why? I'm just me and you're you. This date sounds

amazing."

I shake my head. "It's not that. To me, you're this beautiful woman who has captured my heart with the force of a thousand thundering bulls. I'm trying so hard to impress you. I know the usual wine and dine ain't gonna work with you. You need special but I don't always know what special is... at least I didn't until I met you. When I look at you, Savannah, all reasoning doesn't exist. You're not the typical girl, you're so much more and I want to do everything I can to make you happy and see you smile."

"Well, you're doing a damn good job with that, Cowboy."

I try to hide the devilish smirk, but to no avail. She lightly punches me in the arm and starts laughing. "I only know Sundance; am I riding her?"

"Do you remember how to ride?" I ask, moving Sundance's reins in my hand.

"I do. I rode her the other day."

"You did? Where was I?"

"I'm not sure," she says as her hand trails down the horse's neck. Savannah steps closer and rests her head against the gentle mare. Sundance moves her head slightly, acknowledging Savannah.

I clear my throat. "I was hoping we could ride together."

She nods. "Yeah, I'd like that," she says seductively.

It doesn't register what she just said until I see her mount Sundance. I quickly move and heave myself up behind her. Still holding the reins, we trot off toward the river that we have to cross to get to the pond. I've known this land for most of my life and I still haven't been to every part.

Savannah leans back against me, allowing me to guide

our way. Having her in front of me like this is indescribable. I can't get enough of her and I know it's dangerous, but right now I'm willing to accept the consequences.

When we get to the river, I feel her freeze. I stifle a laugh, as Sundance knows just what to do and starts walking across.

"It's so beautiful out here."

"Nothing's as beautiful as you."

She giggles and tells me to stop it. I won't ever.

"Sometimes I think I want to build a property out there but then I'd have to build a bridge and put a driveway through the land. It'd ruin it. I could always just ride out there, but you can only do so much on a horse, ya know?"

"You could build a cabin and pretend you're on vacation."

"I could," I say just as we climb the hill leading to the pond. The sun is casting the perfect glow and I have a feeling the water is going to be the right temperature at this time of night. As soon as Sundance brings us to the crest I know what I want to do next and once again the ideal date in my mind could be shot to hell.

"Want to go swimmin'?"

"What?" she scoffs. "I don't have my suit and where would we go?"

The pond comes into view and from where we are the sun is casting an orange glow over the valley.

"I thought we could swim here and I'm fairly certain no one is going to see us."

Savannah looks around and turns slightly to look at me. "You know, I think I do want to go swimming."

Hallelujah! I scream on the inside. Now the only question left to answer is – what will she wear?

Chapter Sixteen

Savannah

*T*yler helps me off Sundance and right into his arms. I let my hands slide ever so slowly over his shoulders before taking off his hat, setting it on my head as I wink at him. He presses his lips to mine, his tongue moving fluidly with mine. He holds me in his arms with his hand spread across my back, keeping me pressed tightly against his chest. My legs wrap around his waist causing my dress to bunch. Had I known we were heading out on the horses, I would've changed into shorts. Somehow I have a feeling that Tyler didn't want me to know and I'm okay with that.

His lips move to my shoulder as his arm goes under me for support. I want to kiss him back but his hat is blocking me. The thought of taking it off now that I have it on doesn't appeal to me, but I need to kiss him.

"Leave it on," he mumbles against my skin as if he's reading my mind. The words sexy, beautiful and gorgeous are coming out of his mouth and each word ignites a slow burn inside of me. The strap on the dress is slowing being moved down my shoulder.

"I need to stop before I do something we're not ready for." He sets me down gently even though I'm not ready to let him go. I pull my bottom lip in between my teeth to keep from balking. "God, you look sexy in my hat. Are you sure I can't buy you one?"

I shake my head, pursing my lips. "I like yours just fine."

"Of course you do," he says, playfully. "Do you want to eat first or go for a swim? The pond is warm, and it's clean. Jeremiah ran a pump to keep the water fresh."

My eyes fall upon the pond and notice there's a beach-like landing. "What about fish? I'd really hate to get bitten by a fish."

Tyler laughs as he steps away and starts unbuttoning his shirt. I've seen him almost naked, but standing here, watching, makes my heart beat a little faster. A gentle warmth spreads across my stomach, causing my cheeks to flush, and I bite down on my tongue and twist my hands together to keep from reaching out to touch him. He kicks off his boots and pulls his belt loose. I focus on his fingers as they undo each button on his jeans. He removes his shirt, letting it drop to the ground. I look around for any prying eyes or Jeremiah. I wouldn't put it past him to follow us out here.

"No one here but us, sweetheart."

"And Sundance," I add for good measure.

"She's not going anywhere."

"Well, that's good to know," my voice cracks and even though I want to be here with him, I'm nervous.

Tyler pushes his pants down, letting them pool at his

ankles. He hops on one foot while trying to remove each pant leg. I laugh and cover my mouth.

"Darlin', I can assure you that looked a lot sexier in my head."

"You're sexy," the words pour out of my mouth before I can stop them. His eyes widen and I know there's no taking it back. I don't want to. Tyler's eyes gleam as he steps forward and I try to keep my eyes focused on his, but they trail down his chest and below his waist. His dark briefs are holding back his bulge. I take a deep breath at the realization that I make him that way. That knowledge alone is exhilarating. My body temperature rises. Even in this heat I can feel myself getting hotter, even though I get goosebumps when he brushes up against me.

"Savannah," he whispers huskily as his hands trail up my arms and over my shoulders. My head turns slightly to watch him pull down the thin straps of my dress. They rest just above my elbow and I know he's waiting for me to take the next step. I turn, pulling my hair to the side and wait.

Tyler's lips dance along my skin while his fingers pull the zipper down. I don't know how far we're going tonight but everything feels right. Being out here, in the open with him... this is where I'm meant to be.

His hands gently push my straps down, allowing the dress to settle at my feet. "Can I see you, Savannah?" he asks, with his chest touching my back. I nod and step out of my dress to turn and face him. I'm bare-chested with nothing but panties and boots on and the man in front of me is mesmerized by me. My face flushes as he takes me in. I try to cover myself, feeling self-conscious, but he holds my hands in his.

"You're the most beautiful woman I've ever seen."

"Thank you." My response seems lacking, but he'll never understand the magnitude of that compliment. After being called a slut and a whore by my friends, he's working to reverse the damage that has been done and doesn't even realize it.

"What do you say we go for a dip in the pond before we eat? It's blazing out here and I think we could both cool off a bit. Besides, we're both almost naked and it seems like the best thing to do," he chuckles lightly.

I agree and slip off my boots before taking his hand. He leads us to the edge and kisses me lightly before pulling us into the water.

Tyler and I hold each other in the pond, basking in the mellowness of the water. We're all lips and hands as we make-out in the water. I love being in his arms and know I want to take things further with him. I don't want him to be hesitant or afraid I might rebuff him, I won't. I'm just not sure how to tell him.

The pond is refreshing and a welcome relief from the heat. I thought when I arrived, I'd hate it here. Truth is I'd take Rivers Crossing over New York City any day. There's so much freedom to be who you are without being someone fake. I'm not blind; I know people judge you no matter where you live but at least here, with Tyler, Jeremiah and my aunt and uncle, I'm not judged because of what I did.

When we get out, dripping wet and rejuvenated, Tyler pulls a blanket from the horse and lays it on the ground. I pick up his shirt and slip it on, leaving the top buttons undone. He sets out our food and while it all looks delicious, I want something else from him... but only after I tell him how I feel and what's weighing on my mind.

Sitting cross-legged in front him, his eyes widen when he takes in my attire. He trails his index finger down the exposed valley of my breasts. Everything I experienced in New York has been nothing compared to the way Tyler is with me.

"I have something to tell you and I'm not sure how to say it. Actually, it's a couple of things."

"You can tell me anything," he says as he moves closer to me. His fingers caress my skin and he laughs when it pebbles.

"Well..." I start, wringing my hands together. "I want to be with you."

"I want to be with you too, Savannah, but we don't have to rush anything. I like that we're taking our time and getting to know each other. I love that I'm learning your body and figuring out what turns you on. You fascinate me in the best way."

When he admits to romantic disclosures like that, it makes the next part so hard to say. "We don't have time," I spit out.

His hand stalls on my leg and his brow furrows. "What do you mean?"

"My mom... she called last night, I leave for Paris next week."

Tyler sits up immediately and I feel the loss of his touch as if he's stabbing me in the heart. He shakes his head. "Why?"

"I don't know. The last time we talked she said I'd be lucky to survive the summer, but she called and told me that she made arrangements for me to go earlier. I told her I didn't want to, but she's not listening to me." I crawl on my knees to Tyler and place my arms around him. "I don't want to go, but I do. I've wanted to study in Paris for so long."

He nods. "It's a good thing for you, Savannah." He turns and pulls me into his arms. "I'll miss you though, something fierce."

"Me too," I reply, as I lean forward and kiss him. This time he doesn't hold back and reclines. I shift so that I'm lying over the top of him and it's only seconds before I feel his need pressing against me. I sit up and unbutton his shirt. Tyler watches my every move. The moment his shirt is off me, he's maneuvered so he's on top, resting on his arms so that he's hovering over me.

"I'm afraid that I'm falling hard for you."

"Me too," my voice breaks, as I look into his eyes. He takes me all in, his eyes never leaving me as he sits back on his knees, hooking his fingers into my panties and sliding them down my leg.

"I want this with you, Savannah. But if you don't want to, just tell me to stop and I will."

I shake my head. "I want this. I want you, too."

He nods and reaches for his jeans, pulling out the square package that will take us past the point of no return. He shimmies out of his boxer briefs and sheaths himself, hovering over me, his lips finding mine as he makes us one.

Chapter Seventeen

Tyler

*I*t's been a week since Savannah told me the devastating news. I had to hold back my emotions when she informed me that she was leaving early. I couldn't let her know that I was breaking inside and each day since, I've done everything I can to show her how much she means to me. Each night when I lie in bed and listen to the hum of the air conditioner, unable to fall asleep, I wonder if it'd be so bad if I drove us to Vegas to get married. Right now, I'm willing to be as non-traditional as possible if it means she stays.

As much as I want to keep her here, I can't. Doing so makes me no better than her momma. I want to be the one person who doesn't let Savannah down and the only way to do that is to keep up my façade that I'm okay, even when I'm dying on the inside.

Never in a million years did I think I'd feel like this, especially when she stepped off the bus. Her attitude was such a turn off that I thought for sure we'd continue to butt heads, but she surprised me over and over again. The reemergence of the Savannah that I grew up with was just waiting to be triggered and when she finally started to show, she blew me away. She just needed to remember who she was and now that it's finally happened, she's leaving me all too soon.

I'm supposed to have months, not weeks and now only hours. This goodbye isn't supposed to happen until late August, but once again her momma is taking her away from me and this time I know I won't see her again. I have no doubt she'll meet her soul mate in Paris and fall in love under the Eiffel tower, forgetting what it's like to live here. She won't need me, not as much as I need her. Savannah McGuire has my heart. She'll be boarding a plane with it in her hand and there ain't jack shit I can do about it. Asking her to stay won't do. I can't ask her to give up her dreams for me. I have nothing to offer her except for me and I fear that I'm not enough.

Resting my head against the steering wheel, I take a deep breath in an effort to calm my anxiety. Savannah thinks I'm going to drive her into town to catch the bus. That doesn't work for me. I'll be driving her to Austin and waiting with her until the very last possible minute. I know I'm torturing myself, but I can't help it. I don't want to let her go. It's selfish of me to feel this way, but I just got her back and I'm not ready to lose her.

I reluctantly start my truck and shift it into drive. My hand hangs over the top of the wheel as I navigate the main road back to the ranch. I could've driven through the road we created when I moved in but it shortens my trip and I'm not ready to load Savannah's bags into the back of my truck.

All too soon I'm pulling into the long driveway that

leads to the house. Putting my truck into park, I refuse to shut off the engine. I wish I knew a way to stop this, but I don't. The moment Savannah climbs into my truck for the last time, our lives are going to be forever changed.

Savannah steps out with her stupidly big purse and her suitcase behind her. I close my eyes, hopeful that something, anything, will come to mind to make this moment go away. I slam my shoulder into my door, pushing it open. I can't make eye contact with her as I take the steps two at a time, but when I'm there in front her I waste no time placing my lips against hers. My hands cup her face, holding her to me. Today, I need to call the shots and be as physical as I can with her. I need the memory of her lips ingrained in my mind.

I hate that I have to pull away, but standing on this porch waiting for the inevitable to catch up with me is pointless. With another brush of my lips against hers, I pull away. My heart breaks at the sight of tears slowly falling down her cheeks. My thumbs wipe them away as I lean my forehead against hers.

Clearing my throat, I step away and pick up her suitcase. It's lighter than I thought, giving me hope that she's left some of her clothes here for when she returns. Lord knows I'm praying that she does. Savannah follows behind, climbing in and slamming her door. I hope that it's pent up anger from leaving that she's taking out on my truck.

When I come around to my side, I open the door to find her in the middle. I smile at her. She doesn't know how much this small gesture means to me. I'm thankful we're leaving so early so I can drive the back roads, because taking the highway and making her move away from me is not an option.

I climb in and hold her hand as her head rests on my shoulder. I'm afraid the ride is going to be done in silence and that's not what I want. I want to hear her voice and record it for my memories. It's my choice to live out in the sticks and right now I'm willing to give up my house for an apartment with Internet. Phone calls are going to get very expensive. That's if she calls me.

"Where we going?" she asks, as we pass the solitary bench in the middle of nowhere. The same place where I picked her up not so many weeks ago.

"I'm not letting you take the bus to Austin. I'm driving you."

"Tyler, you don't have to."

Doesn't she know that right now I'd do whatever she wanted me to? If she asked me to go to Paris, I'd do it in a heartbeat... but she won't. She either doesn't want to interrupt my life or doesn't want me in hers. I'm praying it's the former because not having her in mine isn't going to be easy.

"I know I don't have to, but I need to be with you until the very last second."

"Thank you," she says through her tears. I put my arm around her and relax into the seat so she can snuggle into me some more. She grips my shirt and sobs, killing me slowly with each and every shake of her body. I have to bite my lips to keep my own tears at bay. Savannah won't see me cry. Maybe when she's out of sight and I'm pulled off onto the side of the road I'll let out some frustrations, but not in front of her. I, at least, need to try and be strong for the both of us.

The drive is shorter than I had hoped and when I pull into the airport parking lot, we're both quiet. I shut off the truck and wrap my arms around her, kissing her neck, cheeks, eyes and finally her lips.

"I hate that our summer was cut short," I whisper against her mouth. I honestly don't know what else to say to her, except to ask her to stay, but I have nothing to offer her. She doesn't need to be tied down to some ranch hand. This is the life I chose for me, she didn't choose it for her. Her dreams are far too important to her and to me. She needs this opportunity to grow.

"I love you, Tyler."

My heart stops at those three little words that mean so much. I pull back from her to look in her eyes. I can tell by the shine in them that she means it. She loves me.

"I love you, Savannah, so much. It's so hard not to and, believe me, I tried."

We hold each other and spend most of our time kissing until it's time for her to go. I hold her hand as we walk through the airport, dragging her suitcase behind us. It's only when she has her ticket in hand that I feel my throat closing up. I can't cry in front of her. I just can't.

Savannah falls into my arms when we reach security. Her body shakes with sobs. I hold her to me, trying to take away her pain but my own is just as present. I can't help but wonder if she'd be like this at the end of the summer or if we'd be okay with saying goodbye. Something tells me things would be worse.

Savannah pulls me down for a kiss, this time her hands cupping my face. She peppers me with kisses, telling me that she loves me once again. Before I can reply, she's running up to the TSA agent and checking in. All I can do is stand there and watch her disappear from me.

I move to the side where I can have a better view of

her and wait for her to turn around. I tell myself if she does I'm going to ask her, no beg her, to stay... to stay and be with me.

Except she doesn't turn around and I can no longer see her.

She's gone.

Chapter Eighteen

Savannah

The lights, sounds and people are why I'm here. Seeing the pictures and videos from my mother's trips over the past few years has been what's encouraged my yearning to spend time in Paris. My mom has been able to travel since she took the job in New York and I've always wanted the same experience. The difference with me is I want to do mine before starting college or settling down. It's important for me to be different from my mother and not follow her path in life. At times while growing up, I've felt she resents my dad for dying so young and leaving her as a single mom working her way through college. Now I'm just in her way. Instead of demanding I go to college and work toward a sustainable career, like a levelheaded parent would, she sends me away.

It's been a month since I've left Tyler, the ranch and my aunt and uncle behind. Regret and longing weigh heavily on my mind, but I'm torn. I'm where I want to be, where I dreamed of being for so long, yet Paris doesn't seem to fit me the way I thought it would. The shopping, the cafés, and the museums are everything I wanted, but I can't help but feel that something's missing. I don't know if it's Tyler, Aunt Sue, the ranch or even Jeremiah that's missing. It may even be that I don't fit anywhere, and this is my mind's way of telling me to keep searching.

I miss Tyler, more than I thought I would. I constantly wonder what he's doing and if he's met someone. It's not fair of me to hope that he hasn't, but I'd like to think that he's waiting. We haven't spoken much. There have been a few emails here and there, but no declarations of undying love, except for the occasional 'I love you'. I'm okay with that though because I'm here and he's there... we're on different paths, I guess you'd say. Mine is one of self-discovery of whom or what I'm supposed to be and his is taking over my uncle's farm and hanging out with Jeremiah at Red's. I can't really fault him, there have been a few times since being here I dreamt of being back on the ranch, hearing Jeremiah tease me, or having one of my aunt's freshly baked pies.

It's the little things in life that you take for granted. Like the smell of clean linen when it's hung on the line to dry, freshly cut grass, a horse giving you a kiss because you've cleaned his stall. I didn't realize how much those simple acts meant to me until I returned to the bustling city.

Now my days are spent walking around and exploring. It was my mother's grand idea to have me live with a colleague of hers, saying that it's better than living in a hostel. That's what I wanted. I wanted to be free and live sparingly. My new babysitter is Alexis. She's single, has never been married and has no children. She's a replica of my mother, working long hours and never home. On my first weekend here, she showed me around. We drove to the countryside, hit the high fashion boutiques, ate lunch on the Seine and I naively thought things would be different here. I had visions of us doing something together every weekend, even meeting for dinner at a small café. I was wrong and was pretty much told to fend for myself. It's like living in New York, except I'm in Paris eating croissants instead of bagels and trying to understand a foreign language. It's the place I've wanted to be for the past few years, yet I find myself wishing I were in Texas.

My days consist of being a tourist. I've told myself that I need to take advantage of my free time and if Alexis isn't free, I'll do it myself. On the list today is the Eiffel tower. Yesterday was the Louvre. Each day is something new because of the long lines to get in. I don't have the money to pay for a guided tour, even though I've thought about hopping on one of those high school tours that are all over the place. I honestly don't think anyone would know that I didn't belong and I want the amenities that come with it. They aren't waiting in hours of long lines or being shuffled off to the side so others can get through first.

I thought about calling my mom and asking for the money to take a guided tour, but that would only lead to an in-depth conversation about college. When am I applying and to where and if fashion is still my direction? College is only on my mind when I'm lying in bed at night, thinking about Tyler. He's taken just enough schooling so he can run the ranch when my uncle hands it over to him. He likes things simple, whereas I want them complicated. For the past few years, my life has been a revolving door of high society drama. Who kissed whom? Who slept with so- and- so's boyfriend. Or did you hear blah blah got caught snorting coke? It was as if the drama was needed like a double shot from Starbucks. Even though I haven't spoken to any of my friends from New York since I left, it doesn't mean I haven't kept up on the soap opera known as Facebook. On there, I'm invisible, yet active with my status updates and ridiculous emojis as responses. It's enough to keep the ties loose but with enough slack that I can pull away if need be.

With no funds for that guided tour, I'm stuck like the commoner I am, in line for the tower. I think I've moved about an inch in the past hour, waiting for my turn to go to the second floor. I'm hoping that by the time I get there, it'll be dusk and I can just stand and watch the lights shine over the city. Being in Texas for a short time has made me realize how much I've not only missed, but also didn't take advantage of, when I was living in the city. Sightseeing is something you do with your grandparents when they come to visit, not with your girlfriends, unless it's walking down Fifth Avenue. I never went to the Empire State Building willingly and now I wish I had.

Using only my peripheral vision, I take a tiny step forward. My nose has been buried in my novel all morning and afternoon. I read more to pass the time. Tomorrow I'm taking the train to the country simply because I have yet another book to read. They're crazy smut novels, only designed to increase my longing for Tyler. I don't care though. I need them to pass the time. It's either this or sitting at a café in a metal chair watching the women walk along the cobblestone roads in ridiculous heels. I've bellowed out a few laughs at their attempts to be sexy. Thing is, that was me a few months ago and it still would've been me had I not detoured to the ranch where I was reeducated on what it's like to be a real girl, one that can dress-up and isn't afraid to get dirty. It's not the clothes that make you sexy it's your attitude and zest for life. Your willingness to learn something new.

I'm bumped from behind and mutters of an apology are spoken in English. The man behind me is swearing profusely and trying to figure out how to tell me he's sorry in French. I wish he wouldn't. I close my book and turn around to tell him that it's okay. A soft smile and a relieved look spread across his clean-shaven face. He's wearing an Army green colored shirt and shorts. Thankfully his feet are covered in Nikes and not sandals with socks. I don't know who came up with that fashion, but it needs to leave and never return. Ever!

"I'm sorry," he says again with a grimace. I'm gathering he thinks I'm French, which is odd since we're at one of the largest tourist traps in the world and I don't believe Parisians even visit unless they're doing the obligatory sightseeing trip with family.

"It's no problem," I say in perfect English. "I won't be the last person you bump into while you're visiting."

"You speak English!" His excitement is catching and I find myself happily giggling. Something I haven't done since I arrived. His hand runs over his hat giving me a glimpse of what I gather is a shaved head. It's a gesture that reminds me not only of Tyler, but Jeremiah as well. You know you're homesick when you're missing someone like Jeremiah Moore.

"I'm Savannah," I say as I reach out to shake his hand. I dropped the Vanna act because Tyler and Jeremiah showed me what an idiot that made me out to be. My mother and Alexis haven't and both say it's what I should go by if I plan to be successful in life.

"I'm Zach," he offers as he slips his hand out of mine. "You're American?"

"Born and bred. I'm on a life finding adventure, I guess you could say." Zach is tall, muscular and very tan. Wherever he was before Paris has done wonders for his skin color. It compliments his brown eyes.

"I'm on leave." He nods toward the line and after a quick glance I realize that I've held us up. The last thing I need is for the tourists to start a riot. Everyone needs to get to the second and third floors for their most magical proposals and if they're not already nervous enough, me holding up the line isn't helping.

"What branch?" Months ago I wouldn't have known what to ask. Months ago I wouldn't have asked. My friends would've been with me and on him like vultures. That's how we are... or how they are. My position on romance and life has changed drastically and while I'm not perfect, I'm trying.

"Marines," he offers, with another nod toward the moving line. I figure that's my cue to move the line forward and maybe stop talking. I open my book and pick up from the top of the page.

"Where are you from?"

For the first time since arriving I'm about to engage in a conversation with someone who wants to know about me. Maybe I'm being presumptuous, but I have nothing to lose. I slip my closed book into my bag and angle myself just right so I can talk to Zach and watch the line.

"I'm originally from Texas, but have been living in New York City for a while. What about you?"

"I'm stationed just outside San Diego."

It doesn't escape my notice that he doesn't tell me where he's from, only where he lives. Maybe I'm too presumptuous in thinking that he wants to talk to me, or maybe I'm just to eager to have someone to talk to.

"Have you ever been there?" he asks.

I shake my head quickly and move forward again. We're both able to board the same elevator to take us to the second floor. He stands next to me, his arm grazing against mine. I'm half expecting to feel something a jolt or excitement of some sort but I don't and it could be because I'm not looking for it. Tyler and I are just friends and even though I'm in love with him, we're different and thousands of miles away from each other.

"How long are you in France for?"

"Two weeks," he says. "I just got off the plane this morning."

Before I know what I'm saying, the idea in my head is now falling from my lips. "I'm new here and am sight-seeing myself. Maybe we can do it together."

Zach's smile is brilliant and reaches his eyes. "I'd like that."

Chapter Nineteen

Tyler

*J*eremiah Moore is the epitome of an asshole. He knows I'm missing Savannah and instead of being my best friend and helping me overcome my magnitude of grief, the jerk has made a playlist for when we're together. He's even gone as far as changing one particular song to the text tone on his cell phone. Being the ladies man that he is, his phone is constantly going off so all I hear, every single time we're together is the annoying voice of Madonna repeating "time goes by so slowly". Jeremiah is lucky I'm not a hunter.

It's funny. Savannah wasn't here all that long for me to become attached, except I did. Aunt Sue says it's because her and I are meant to be together, we just haven't found the right time yet. I can neither agree nor disagree. When Savannah left, my heart was ripped right out of my chest and fed to the wolves. For the first time ever, I called out sick, telling Bobby that I just couldn't work because I had the flu or something equally ridiculous. I stayed in bed and held the pillow she used to my face, inhaling her scent. I didn't do that stupid shit when Annamae and I broke up, so I couldn't understand why I was doing it now.

My momma put it in perspective. Savvy coming back was the closure I needed when she left the first time. She said had she never left, this is what I'd be going through- if not worse- when she'd be headin' to college.

Thing is, not a lot of folks from Rivers Crossing, Texas head to college unless we're playing football. I didn't play, and neither did Jeremiah. Most girls around here try out for the cheer team, or whatever it's called, in hopes to land a husband. Thinking Savannah would've been like that is hard. I picture her mounted on a horse, herding cattle or driving the tractor.

While we were growing up she was Uncle Bobby's sidekick when she wasn't with me and Jeremiah. Aunt Sue was teaching her how to cook until she had to move away. So no, I don't necessarily agree with momma, at least on the college part. I do think it's been the closure I need, just not sure it's what I wanted.

Talking to her on the phone is hard. The time difference is difficult to figure out. Email is easier, but my computer is so damn old it takes ages to turn on and the Internet out here isn't that fast, so sending her a diary of my life can't really happen. The few times we've spoken, it's been short and sweet. She asks about her aunt and uncle, I tell her they're good. I ask about Paris, she sighs and says she's learning. Before you know it, the time is up on my calling card and we're saying that we miss each other before the line goes dead.

I looked into getting an iPhone, but with the lack of

Internet on the ranch, it's pointless. Sort of like my relationship with Savannah. I love her and know she loves me, but we can't make this work if we can't communicate. It seems we're only able to be together if she's here and I don't have a clue as to when she's coming back... if she even is. She left all her "ranch" clothes behind and took just her city life with her. It's as if she's closing this door on her life. Not that I blame her.

Della slides me a fresh beer. The frothy foam spills over the rim and I use the rag she keeps on the bar to clean it up. Each night after work I'm in here. Each night I leave by myself. The girl I want is currently five thousand two hundred miles from me, living the life she had planned out until one night screwed that up for her. If she hadn't screwed up, she would've never come to Texas and I wouldn't be sitting here drinking my sorrows away.

Every song that plays on the jukebox sparks a reminder of Savannah. It could be anything from long legs, picnic lunches or bonfires. She and I didn't do much while she was here, but the things we did do created a lifetime of memories. At least they did for me. Each song reminds me of what a cliché I've become as I sit at the same bar night after night, drinking the same type of beer over and over again.

I'm a bad country song waiting to happen.

Jeremiah walks in without an entourage. It's shocking to see, more so because he's had a new friend every night of the week recently. I swear he's running a dating business out of Red's because women are flocking here to meet him. It's like he's famous or something. I don't get it. He's just a straight up backwards talking cowboy and women are chasing him like he's the keeper of the golden ticket to Willy Wonka's Chocolate Factory.

He slaps me on the back just as I'm about to take a drink. Beer sloshes and wets the front of my shirt. "Asshole," I mutter as he sits down.

A few times since Savannah left, I thought about finding a new bar to drown my sorrows in because after working with Jeremiah all day and hanging with him at night, I get my fill. I'm tired of hearing that I need to let go, move on and nail the next piece of ass that walks through the door or shows up to buy hay from us. It's not how I operate. Never has been. When Annamae left me for the greener pastures of Rufus, I didn't start sleeping around. Hell I didn't even care. That's what tells me that shit between Savannah and I was real. I care that she's gone. I care that I haven't been able to speak with her every night. We were just getting started and deserve a chance to get together... if that's what she wants.

This is where everyone cheers for me and tells me to go get the girl. Yee-haw and all that happy horse shit. In order to do that, I need a passport and I don't have a clue as to how I get one.

THE SCREEN DOOR slams behind me and the clatter of silverware against glass tells me that I've interrupted supper. One doesn't simply interrupt supper at the McGuires's – if you show up, you stay and eat. By the time I'm walking into the dining room, Sue is up and in the kitchen already fixing me a plate. I'll never have the heart to tell her I just ate, or that my appetite hasn't been the same since Savannah left because I'm afraid of hurting her feelings. Aunt Sue can cook and no man in the surrounding next ten counties over will pass up a meal fixed by her.

Fried chicken, greens and fresh corn on the cob are set down in front of me. I haven't been around as much, aside from work, and she knows why. It's hard and we both miss Savvy. It's just easier to stay busy and away from people who want to talk about her. Except for tonight.

Before I can muster up the courage to ask for help, I dig in and let the wholesome goodness soak up the beer that's festering in my gut. After a few bites and a nice ice-cold glass of milk to wash it down, I look at her aunt and uncle and prepare myself.

"I want to go to Paris and get Savannah."

Aunt Sue gasps, but Uncle Bobby sets his fork down calmly and wipes his face on his sleeve.

"What makes you think she'll come back with you, boy?"

Boy. Not son. Not Tyler, but boy. The overprotective side of him is showing in spades. It's fine. He can be like that, but I'm an adult and Savannah will be one soon. Once she's eighteen her mother can't tell her what do anymore.

"I don't, but I want to try."

"You gonna make an honest woman out of her?"

"Bobby," Sue scolds, but he's right and he also just showed his hand. Savannah and I kept our relationship a secret. The only two who knew were Aunt Sue and Jeremiah. Neither of them would've sold us out, especially Jeremiah. He may be a gossip, but only when it's for his benefit. Getting me fired, or having Savannah sent away wouldn't aid him in any way. For the life of me I couldn't understand why her mother suddenly had a change of heart about her being here and would send her off to Paris early out of the blue. It's all starting to make sense now –

124

Uncle Bobby knew about Savannah and I and mentioned us when her mother called.

"He's right, Aunt Sue," I reply before turning my attention back to Uncle Bobby. "I imagine in your day, you courted Aunt Sue with the purest intentions. Unfortunately, times have changed and while that is no excuse, Savannah was happy here. Yes, she was looking forward to Paris, but I had a feeling she was going to stay."

"She didn't though," Bobby says, pointing out the obvious since she's not sitting at the table with us now.

"No, she wasn't given a choice."

"You plan to give her a choice?" his voice is booming and authoritative. I've never really seen this side of Bobby before and honestly it scares me a bit. He's giving new meaning to shaking in my boots.

"Of course I do. It's not like I'm going to go over there and drag her back, kicking and screaming."

Sue puts her hand on Bobby's wrist to get his attention.

"Bobby, he's not asking for your permission, he's asking for our help. We need to give it to him." She's right. I do need their help. I don't know how to get a passport, not that I'm expecting either of them to, but Sue will know someone who knows someone. That's how small towns work.

I love Bobby, but the overbearing uncle attitude needs to go. She's almost an adult and can make her own decisions. If I get there and she's happy, fine. I'll leave, but not after I've had my say.

"Thanks, Aunt Sue." I get up and give her a kiss on the cheek. I feel her smile and hope that if Savannah and I are lucky enough to be together in the future, she's soft and gentle like her aunt... although her aunt is really one in a million.

Chapter Twenty

Savannah

Zach and I walk back to his hostel together under a cloud of darkness. We're side by side but there is enough distance between us that everything is casual. He offered to walk me home, but I'm still a city girl through and through and know that it's dangerous to let a stranger know where you live. Besides, if he's in the right place at the right time, he'll see me coming out the door. Definite drawback to living on the Champs de Elysees: You can't hide from the tourists and according to Zach's schedule he'll be on my street in three days.

He complained, but I wouldn't budge. I'm not the kind of girl who tells a guy she just met at the Eiffel Tower where she lives. In my romance novel, it sounds great. In the crime report, it's an act of stupidity.

We stayed on the second floor of the tower, exploring each side of Paris together. It's nice that he lives by the same map I do, although I wish it were a year from now and I were meeting him, or someone similar, so I could be a proper host. It makes me wonder if Tyler will visit, or if the only time I'll see him again is if I go back to Texas. I'm not sure I can. I've wanted Paris for so long I feel as if I have to make it work.

I haven't really enjoyed being here before as I much as I have today. It was good to laugh and even cry a little at some of the jokes Zach was telling. But each emotion brought back a memory of Tyler and I often found myself comparing him to Zach. Would Tyler let me drag him around from museum to museum? Would he want to walk along the Seine and over the aptly named Love Locks Bridge and see the few padlocks that remain? Or would he only want to spend his time here out in the country, looking at the vast green pastures and learning how people farm here?

Tyler is a wild horse in my life or maybe I'm the free spirit that can't be tamed in his. I know he'd be there for me, but I'm not sure our lifestyles can blend. After seeing the lights of Paris for this past month, watching the people as they rush from place to place, and listening to the cars at night – the city is what I love. It tells a story, the people are its chapters. The country is nice for a break, but I'm not sure it'll ever measure up to what I'm seeing now.

By the time we reach the third floor the sun has set and just like every other night in Paris, wedding proposals are being made. People clap, cheer and offer well wishes to the soon-to-be betrothed. Zach and I make it a game. Walking around pointing at which couple we think will be next. It's very hit or miss, but an overall enjoyment for our evening. Of course we get more wrong than right, but we aren't really counting.

Zach thanks me when we stop at the hostel. It's that awkward   we-just-met-should-I-give-you-a-hug-or-give-you-my-number moment. He opts for the hug, pulling me into his muscular arms, which only serve to remind me of Tyler. I should call him when I get home, but that means stopping at the corner store and buying a phone card. And the fact that I'm making up excuses or reasons why we shouldn't talk is stupid and a complete eye opener. If he wanted to be with me, he would've asked me to stay, right? I pat Zach on the back and he lets go. "Are you sure you're okay to walk home? I'm having a hard time letting you go on your own. It's dangerous out there."

I look up and down the street and shrug. "I'll be fine."

He nods, but the frown he has doesn't dissipate. "Here's my number," he says as he pulls my hand out and writes it on my forearm. Smart, this way the sweat on my palms won't make the ink wash off.

I agree and tell him that I'll see him bright and early for our countryside train ride. The novel that I was planning on reading tomorrow will just have to wait.

"It was very nice meeting you Zach." I walk away before he can say anything and I definitely don't turn around to see if he's watching me. It's killing me not to, but it's far too soon for anything like that, plus my head is in a fog. If anything, Zach will be a fun companion until his journey is over and he's back doing whatever it is that he does.

As soon as I'm home with the doors locked, I pull out my phone and text him. The conversation bubble pops up immediately. I can't help but smile at the thought that he was waiting for me. Either that or he was texting his friends back home and I just interrupted. Regardless, he tells me good night and that he's excited for tomorrow.

That makes two of us.

I STOP at the café on the corner and order the same thing I do every day, black coffee with milk and sugar... a lot of sugar. Each time I order it, the barista gives me a strange look. It's almost as if they're confused on how to just pour a cup of coffee and simply add milk and sugar instead of adding nine other things to it. As soon as the hot paper cup is in my hand, I'm out the door and heading toward Zach's hostel. I'm not much of a coffee drinker, but everyone in Paris is and I don't want to stand out. I even sit and drink it out of tiny cups with my pinky in the air. It's something everyone should do when they're in Paris.

It doesn't take me long to reach the hostel and when I get there, Zach is standing outside with his foot resting against the wall. Tyler sometimes stands like that. Thoughts of Tyler cause me to stop short and focus on a leaf that is mindlessly swirling on the ground. Everything reminds me of Tyler and I know that's the way it should be, but each moment is painful. I don't want to live like that.

"Good morning," Zach says, breaking my reverie. "Did you bring me one?"

"What?" I look at him, confused, and see that he's pointing to my cup of coffee. It dawns on me that I should've grabbed him one or at least texted and ask if he'd like something to drink. "Oh, um... I thought with you being in the service you didn't drink coffee." I'm not exactly quick on my feet, but at least it's something.

Zach laughs and takes the cup from my hand, taking sip. His face scrunches and pushes the cup back into my hands. "I think I'm thankful you didn't bring me a cup. What is that shit?"

"It's my coffee." I laugh and take a sip, not minding the sugar loaded warm breakfast.

"No," he says shaking his head. "That's warm Red Bull on crack. You're in Paris. You're supposed to drink espresso and Frappuccino's."

"Zach, I think you mean I'm supposed to drink the coffee black because in Paris, coffee is like a fine art. Come on, we have a train to catch." I bump his shoulder as I pass by him, heading toward the station.

The train station is busy, but not overly crowded. Zach beats me to the counter and buys our tickets. I try to give him the money, but he's ignoring me, pretending like he can't hear me even though he's smiling. I give up and decide to show him on the large map where we're going today. I point to Vouzeron and drag my finger back to Paris. I don't know what's there, but I've put it on my list of towns to check out.

The public address system announces the train for Chantilly and people rush to the platform.

"Is that our train?" he asks.

"No, it's going in the wrong direction." I show Zach on the map. As soon as my finger points to Chantilly, he grabs my hand and pulls me toward the platform. Before I can ask what's going on, we're on the train, sitting side by side and laughing.

"What's going on?"

He looks around the train with a smile spread across his face. Today his hat is on backwards, but his overall appearance is still the same as yesterday.

"One of the guys at the hostel told me about Chantilly and said that girls really dig it. He said that there's mansions, flowers and some other girly shit so I thought we'd check it out."

"We're in France," I remind him. "There are

131

mansions everywhere. I believe each town has at least one."

"There's also the song. My mom loved that song."

"Loved?" I question.

"She died about ten years ago, cancer. Chantilly is on my list and I'd like to see it with you."

How can I say no? I can't, which is why I sit back in my seat and squeeze his hand. I should let go, but it feels good to hold his hand.

Chapter Twenty-One

Tyler

aking Jeremiah with me to Austin was a mistake. He's like a kid in a candy store, except the adult version. Rivers Crossing is small and definitely behind the times. You won't find a shopping mall, strip mall, chain restaurants or nudie bars. What you do find is good, wholesome cooking, friendly people and land so vast that you can see for miles. In Rivers Crossing, the people are gracious, humble and your best friends within five minutes, unlike the bigger cities. I'm biased, I know.

As I drive around, going from block to block looking for an address that doesn't seem to exist, all I see are food carts and lines of people. Even with my stomach growling it's not enough for me to stop, although I'm half-tempted to because the smells of what's sure to be delicious foods are killing me.

As luck would have it, I'm lost. Aunt Sue worked the phones and the general store like a pro on how to get a passport. When she told me that it'd take six weeks I wanted to kick my ass for waiting so long. It'd be well into two months that Savannah has been gone by the time I could get a little book that allows me to fly over the ocean. But Della told me that you could pay a little extra and get one quicker so that's why I'm in Austin.

What Della didn't tell me was I needed a picture and the lady at the courthouse wasn't too forthcoming with how to find someone who took instant pictures for my application. Hence me being lost in what I'm gathering ain't a great part of town. Jeremiah thinks it's great, though, as he hangs his head out the window yelling yee-haw at people on the street. Right now he's waggling his tongue at the aforementioned nudie bar, which is apparently where he wants to have lunch. I don't know if I should go to the bar or leave Jeremiah there. One decision is surely going to get me in hot water while the other gives me the time I need to get my stuff done. This could be a moment that we look back on in ten years or so and laugh. Depends on if I get the girl or not.

With my pictures, birth certificate, application and checks in hand I stand in line and wait. Who knew getting an emergency passport would be so popular? I didn't, but I also never planned on leaving the country. Savannah's worth it though. I know she's too young to make a commitment like getting married, but just having her here is worth the trip to France. I can't see my life without her in it, even if she's just a neighbor. Thing is, I'm not sure Rivers Crossing is for her and I don't know if the city is for me. My momma said part of being in love is compromise, finding a happy medium for the both of us. I don't know what that would be considering our worlds are vastly different.

Maybe I shouldn't be going after her. I've just about cleaned out my savings to buy a ticket. What if she rejects me? Or has already moved on with some beret wearing French dude? I look down at the paperwork in my hand and sigh. Am I wasting my time?

"You tell her you're coming yet?"

"No," I say with a frown. "Aunt Sue has her address, and she thought it would be 'knight in shining armor' of me to just show up with roses in my hand."

"What if she doesn't need to be saved?"

I glance at Jeremiah and wonder when he became the voice of reason. I'm next in line and starting to sweat, second-guessing what it is that I'm doing. My trip could be futile, or she could come back with me. That's what I want: Savannah back in Texas and living at the ranch. I know that makes me selfish, but she was taken from me once before and I don't want to lose her again.

The lady in front of me is done and now it's my turn. Jeremiah is rocking on the heels of his cowboy boots wondering what I'm going to do. The clerk looks at me, her eyebrows raised and her back hunched. She's already tired from her job of processing applications and I'm holding her up. Stepping forward, it's do or die for me. Jeremiah pats me on the back. I'm not sure if that's encouragement or his way of telling me to get the hell out of here. It's a crap shoot. I know this. She either comes home, or she doesn't. And there's only one way to find out.

My application is stamped, and re-stamped. I'm sure the clerk has worked here long enough that she doesn't have to read or check them. Or maybe she just takes them and some other, higher paid person processes them.

"Seven days," she says without making eye contact

and bellowing out, "next." That's it. I know nothing more or nothing less.

The walk back to the truck is met with Jeremiah going on about something irrelevant to my plight. He means well, but he doesn't get it. He's the guy that refuses to date a girl more than once, even though he's met plenty of upstanding women in his day. Hell, a few of them I'd date if I weren't hung up on a striking blonde who took my heart to Paris with her a month ago.

Getting involved was a mistake. I know this. But it happened and now I'm dealing with the consequences. If her mother hadn't sent her away early, she'd just be getting ready to leave now. I would've used the time given to us wisely and showed her how much Texas means to her. Show her she belongs here and not in some ritzy country where she doesn't speak the language. Make her see I can offer her everything, even when I know in order to do that I have to make a change. Living in a small house on borrowed land isn't what Savannah wants for a future.

I need to be enough for her to want to come home. I'm all I have to offer and even I know it won't be enough.

I'm not happy. Bobby isn't happy. Neither is Jeremiah, but he'll get over it. Bobby on the other hand is ignoring me and barking out orders. I know he's pissed I took the day off to go to Austin. I work six days a week. I've only been sick once and am about to take a vacation. Most employers offer time off in addition to sick time. This is something we were taught in my business class. Bobby is all about business and making sure the ranch is running. I get that. I also get that I shouldn't have taken Jeremiah with me.

We have other employees, but Bobby forgets that.

The ranch is being taken care of, but I'm not here to solve all the problems so he can just work. Jeremiah is going to have to step up his game when I'm gone, otherwise I may not have a job to come back to.

Bobby is gruff. He's a hard worker, but needs to slow down. It's why I went to school, so I can take over the ranch. He just hasn't been willing to let go yet. Maybe that's a good thing considering I'm flying across the world to chase a girl who may not want to be chased.

Orders are barked as soon as Jeremiah and I enter the barn. Tools are being slammed around and curse words muttered. Aunt Sue doesn't like it when we swear, so we try not to, but Bobby doesn't care about that right now. He tells me that the crew on the back forty are hours behind and I need to head out there to find out what's going on. So I do. I have no desire to sit around and be on the receiving end of his death glare.

Being alone in my head is the last thing I need right now, though. All I seem to be able to do is run through all possible scenarios of what could happen when I get to Paris, driving myself crazy. Will she jump in my arms when she sees me? Ask me what I'm doing there? Tell me to go home? It's shitty that out of everything I can think of, I only have one positive thought. I wasn't like this with Annamae and she and I were together a hell of a lot longer than I was with Savannah. Hell, Savvy and I aren't even together. We spent a month making out and a moment having sex by the pond.

The girl is wicked. It's the only way to sum up what I'm feeling. She has a hold on me and I can't seem to break it. I don't remember feeling like this when she left the first time. I know I moped around the house a bit, but

I never asked to go to New York and get her. Probably because I knew she was coming back, or she was supposed to. Each summer Savannah was supposed to come home, but never did. Her mother just left us all behind for her fancy job in the big city and forgot about us.

When I reach the land the other crew is working I can see what Bobby is talking about. The field was mowed days ago and ready for haying this morning, but only one-third of it is done. The guys stop working when they see me pull up in my truck. It's not break time, but they seem to think it is.

I'm angry and frustrated as I slam the door and stalk over to where they're now sitting in the shade.

"Y'all have two hours to finish this field. The bales need to be back to the barn before quitting time."

"It's too hot," one of them says. There are only a few full-time employees; the others come in daily looking for work. Unfortunately, none of my full-timers are in this crew of five. Bad planning on my part and I'll be here all night making sure the job is done because of it.

"Move to Alaska," I say to the group, not caring who is belly aching as I turn away from them. When you live in Texas, it's warm, hot or too hot. You get used to it.

One of them says something about quitting and that's enough for me to lose my cool. I turn back around and look each of them in the eye. Not a single one of them pipes up now and not a single one of them cares.

"You're done for the day. Pay will be ready at five. If you want to get paid, be at the gate."

There's moaning and groaning, inappropriate language being spread around, but I don't care. I hop in the tractor and start getting the job done.

My ticket for France is non-refundable. If I don't go, I lose the money. If I go, I could lose the girl. It's a no win situation and a classic example of thinking with my heart and not my head. Someday, logic will win out, but not today.

Chapter Twenty-Two

Savannah

*L*ast night I dreamt of Tyler. We were sitting in the back of his truck watching the sunset at the beach. His friends were there too, but he and I were lost in our own world. As night fell, he held me under the stars, keeping me warm even though it was still blazing hot outside.

I called him this morning, even though I knew he was sleeping. I secretly had hoped the ringing of the telephone would wake him. I just wanted to hear his voice. When the answering machine came on, I hung up. I don't know why I didn't leave a message, or yell his name so he'd startle awake and rush to the phone. I couldn't bring myself to admit that he's slipping through my fingers.

In a way, coming to France was a mistake. I'm not any closer to figuring out what I want to do here, except sightsee. My heart is torn in half. Part of me wants to go back to Texas and be with Tyler, but I'm afraid of what that means. The reason we left Texas was because my mother wanted something better for us. Could she have gone about it differently, yes, but she did what she felt was right. I don't want to end up like her, pregnant as a teenager and alone. History often repeats itself and that's my fear with Tyler.

The other half of me wants to stay here. I can get lost in the crowd and no one would be the wiser. Yes, school has to happen, but not for a while. I could move to London and study there, or just forgo college and work as a barista. Since meeting Zach, he's opened my eyes to what the world could be. The possibilities are endless and he's right. If I choose not to stay in Paris, it doesn't mean I have to go back to New York or even Texas.

It'd be nice if all the answers to life were written in a book, or displayed in a vending machine. Hit a button and you get the secret to success. Hit another and you'll find true happiness. I think I'll take A7 today and insert my change. My reality is much more bleak, at least for another week. Next week I'll turn eighteen. Zach will still be here, but I haven't told him. He doesn't even know how old I am. He hasn't asked and I haven't volunteered the information that his tour guide is still just seventeen.

Zach is an open book. He was born and raised in Detroit where his father still lives, working as a machinist. His mom died from cancer days after he enlisted in the Marines. He's also on his second tour of duty and ready to be back in San Diego so he can take up surfing. Instead of going home to see his dad, he opted for a vacation away from life.

I don't blame him.

I've seen him every day since we met at the tower. He's fun to be around and I like him. He's different from Tyler and there's a side of me that finds that refreshing. I haven't told him about Tyler, not that I need to. I don't ask Zach if he has a girlfriend because I assume if he did, he'd be with her and not with me. We are in the City of Love after all.

He was only supposed to be in Paris for three days, but decided to stay longer. I tell myself it's because of the magic of Paris and not because of me, but I'm lying to myself. Just as I've been lying to Zach about whom I am. He should know that I'm only seventeen.

Today, I'm full on American. Since I've been here, I've been trying to blend with the Parisians, not today. Ball cap, khaki shorts and a t-shirt. We're going hiking. I'm not a fan, but I'm willing to try anything once. Zach assured me that with his survival skills, if we were to get lost, I'd be in good hands. I fear those hands. I've tried to shy away from physical contact, but it's impossible. I'm gravitating toward him and before I do something stupid, like kiss him, he needs to know everything about me. I vow to make today the day and hope he doesn't leave me in the woods.

Zach knows where I live. It happened just like I thought it would. We were supposed to meet at a café near my house and I was running late. I stepped out, and he just happened to be in front of my door, walking along. He jumped, and I laughed at the absurdity of the situation. I don't mind now that I know him a little better, but it's still awkward. He's ever the gentleman, though, walking me home at night and making sure I get in safely. And in true romantic fashion, I open my window to tell him I made it safely into my apartment instead of texting him.

The first time I did that, I watched him walk away, wishing he were Tyler. I want to be enough for him. I'm just not sure who I am at this point in my life. Tyler knows what he wants – the ranch. He's was born and bred to do that where I wasn't. Every part of Texas was taken out of me when we moved to New York and I don't know if I fit there anymore. I love the solitude that the ranch has to offer, but working there every day is not what I had envisioned for myself.

Zach isn't offering an alternative. I'm not asking him for one either. He is opening my eyes to other possibilities. Making sure I know there's more than just the high society bullshit that my mother spews. Speaking of, I missed my weekly phone call with her and I fear if I don't call her soon, she'll show up. Alexis is none the wiser to my daily activities. She's more absent than my mother is. Score one for Savannah in the parental unit category.

"What happened to your dad?" Zach asks as we walk along the dirt trail. The sun is out, but the temperature is cool. It's perfect hiking weather according to my human survival guide.

I knew it was only a matter of time before Zach would start asking questions about my life. I step off the path and find a place for us to sit overlooking the town we're in. Each town is almost the same, churches, mansions and cobblestone roads. Everything has been preserved inside the smaller towns, but upgraded with modern conveniences.

"I wish I had a life full of memories like you do with your mom. I don't though. I don't even remember my dad. The only way I know what he looks like is through pictures that my aunt and uncle kept. And even those are yellowing from age.

"When I was two, he just didn't come home one day. It wasn't until later, maybe when I was ten or so that my mom told me he had died from cancer. I was just too little to remember the agony he was in, or how sick he was. We lived with my aunt and uncle and my dad was going to take over the ranch when Uncle Bobby died, but once he passed we moved to New York and my mom started over. Even changed her name to something that she deemed more acceptable."

I move some branches with my shoe and gather my thoughts. "Everything that I am today is not who I was supposed to be. My daddy wanted a Southern Belle and so did my mother for a while. I don't know what changed with her or why Rivers Crossing wasn't enough."

"You know the way you just said 'daddy', it's the first time I heard a hint of a southern drawl from you. You're very good at hiding it."

I chuckle and groan. "It's not by choice, believe me. I was as twangy as the girls you see on television, but my mother – who used to be 'Momma' – wouldn't hear of it. She put me in speech classes to remove any signs of Texas. She thought people would look down on us if I didn't pronounce my g's."

"Do you miss Texas?"

What a loaded question that one is. I think about whom I miss, not necessarily the town or the state. If I could put Tyler, Aunt Sue, Uncle Bobby and even Jeremiah in another location, I'd do it in a heartbeat. Thing is, they'd hate New York. Except for maybe Jeremiah. The girls there would flock to him because of his charisma and good looks. He'd just have to bat his eyes, and they'd come running.

"I miss my family, but I'm not a country girl. The idea of waking up before the sun is out doesn't appeal to me.

But the bonfires at night and the stargazing are things I'd never pass up."

"Do you have a lot of friends there?"

I shake my head. I'm sure I would've but I wasn't there long enough to get to know any of my former classmates. "No, just a few," I say without using Tyler or Jeremiah's names. The less he knows the better. It's not like I'll ever see him again after he's gone.

"No boyfriend waiting at home for you?"

"I don't have a home," I tell him. "My mother doesn't want me in New York and she doesn't want me in Rivers Crossing, either. I'm here because she doesn't have to worry about me."

"Let me hear you say something with your accent."

I look at him strangely and wonder if he's mocking me. It's not like people from Michigan don't carry a different dialect. Each region does.

Sighing, I try to think of the most ridiculous thing I can. "I'm fixin' to get all gussied up for the hoedown at the honkytonk." I turn away with embarrassment and cover my face.

"I happen to think Southern girls are cute," he says as he turns me around and pulls my hands away. I wish he hadn't because I know what's coming next. His lips brush against mine while his warm hand caresses my cheek. He doesn't rush nor does he care about the people walking by. His lips are soft, inviting and everything a first kiss shared between two people should be, except this isn't what I want. Any type of first kiss should be met with lightning and fire. When he pulls away, he's smiling.

"We shouldn't do this," I say, watching his face fall.

"Tell me why not."

"Because I'm only seventeen." The words are out of

my mouth before I can sugarcoat them. I could've said it differently, but the verbal vomit has its own ideas. Zach looks away briefly before getting up and heading to the trail. I let him go. He needs to digest what I just told him. From his stories about his life I can easily put him at least at twenty-eight, if not older. A man like him will want nothing to do with a girl like me.

Chapter Twenty-Three

Tyler

$\mathcal{I}$'ve worked my ass off since the day I took off to file my passport application. From sun up to sun down, I'm on the ranch making sure everything is getting done. My nights are now met under the cloak of darkness with critters watching my every move, waiting to come out and scrounge around for rodents and vermin. I'm throwing them off their eating habits, but if I have to suffer, so do they.

The first few nights when I walked into my house, supper was sitting on my table wrapped tightly in aluminum foil. Now Aunt Sue just brings it out to wherever it is I'm working and demands I take a break. I don't know where I'd be without her. Probably wilting away under a tree somewhere, dying of starvation and thirst.

My ass is dead tired and I'm barely hanging on. It's not a good combination for a rancher to be tired and running heavy machinery, but someone has to get the job done... and done right. Jeremiah has his own responsibilities and after I let one crew go last week, I can't afford any more mess-ups. When I do make it to my house, I'm out cold, almost falling asleep in the shower most nights. Even the ringing telephone ain't enough to get me to open my eyes and roll out of bed. I tried, it wasn't gonna happen.

Bobby and I haven't really spoken about my upcoming plans to go to Paris. I don't know if he doesn't want me to go because of the ranch or because he wants me to leave Savannah alone. He hasn't said and I'm not asking. The way I see it, it's my life and I need to know whether to move on or wait. If Savvy tells me to wait, I will because I love her and I know she needs to find herself. But if she tells me to move on, so be it. I can do that and respect the fact that she's asking me to. It's this limbo shit that I can't deal with.

Savannah and I should've resolved everything before she left, but we're young and naïve, thinking we have the whole world and nothing but time ahead of us. Truth is, we do, but we may not be together. I have to know, either way.

Back in the barn, I'm inspecting the stalls, making sure they're cleaned and the horses have fresh hay. The tack room is cleaned and everything put back in place. Bobby hired a young girl who's home for the summer to take care of the horses since Savannah is gone. I think he expected her to be here, just as I did.

It's late and I need to pack, although I know I'm going to stick out like a sore thumb with my cowboy hat and shit kickers. As soon as I step into my house, the AC cools me down but not enough. The shower will take care of the rest. I check the answering machine – no calls. I didn't really expect her call, but had hoped to hear from her. My gut is telling me that she's forgotten about me, moved on.

If she has, I'll have my answer. It'll hurt, but I've been down that road before.

Jeremiah is taking me to the airport. I'm leaving on a red-eye flight and am downright nervous. I've never flown before and a few of the townspeople suggested I fly somewhere small before getting on a transatlantic flight, but I've never had a reason to leave. All the traveling I have to do is done by truck: Auctions, cattle runs, horse swaps. Can't really take a horse on a plane.

The cold water runs through my hair and down my back. Aunt Sue bought me a loofa to use to make sure I'm spic'n span clean when I go to see Savannah. I told her Savannah ain't going to care. She's used to me like this, but Aunt Sue wouldn't hear of it. She even bought me liquid soap that smells like a man, or so she says. I have to admit, after using the loofa, my skin feels pretty good. Not that I'd admit that to anyone else.

I'm packed and pacing the floor, waiting for Jeremiah to get here. I should've driven myself, but instead I listened to Della when she said parking at the airport is a bitch. I hate depending on other people and knowing Jeremiah, he's been out hooking up and has completely forgotten.

I realize he hasn't when I see headlights shining through my window, almost blinding me. Of course, he would have his high beams on just to annoy me. I grab my bag and the present Aunt Sue has for Savannah, making sure my ticket is in my back pocket along with my passport, and head out the door. The fear that's bubbling in my gut is about to drive me crazy. I'll be hurt if she doesn't want me, but it won't be the end of the world. It's not like I haven't lost her before.

At the last minute, I decide to leave my cowboy hat at

home and just take my baseball cap. If I'm going to win her back, or convince her to come home, I need to try and remind her about the good things she's missing, not the things that annoy her. Besides, I don't imagine there are many cowboys in Paris, but you never know.

ONCE I WAS on the plane I knew I was out of my element. Aside from the lack of legroom, the seats are compact, the elderly lady sitting next to me is knitting and asking me if she can use me to measure because I'm just like her grandson, and the flight attendants don't speak English. I'm utterly tired and confused.

Once we've landed, I can't help but think this is all a mistake and I should've just called her and made her have the conversation on the phone instead of coming over here. I'm lost and following the crowd out of the airport. Per Della's suggestion, I brought a carryon. I packed what I could in this suitcase, borrowed from her, so I wouldn't have to wait for my luggage. I'll have to kiss her when I get home as a thank you. I'm grateful for her advice.

Tour buses, taxicabs and black cars line the parking area in front of the airport. I haven't a clue as to where I'm going, aside from having Savannah's address on a piece of paper, and I'm not sure how to get there. I fear I'm quickly going to lose it and all I want to do right now is turn around and get on the plane back home. This place isn't for me. I should've spent the last week learning French instead of working until my fingers bled.

Somehow I thought there would be subtitles, but I don't know why. It's not like English has ever been the official language of France, so why should they cater to us Americans? They shouldn't. It's me who has to adapt, but

I'm an idiot. I need to wear a sign on my shirt that says, "Stupid American looking for his girlfriend," and maybe someone would be gracious enough to help me.

"You need help?" I turn at the sound of a man voice behind me. His English is broken, but it's enough for me to understand.

"Yes, please." Pulling out the paper that has Savannah's address on it, I hand it over and he smiles. I take that as a sign that he can help me. He nods toward the taxicab and tells the driver where to take me. All I know to do is to shake his hand and tell him thank you.

I'm holding on for dear life. I think this driver took lessons from Jeremiah. Taxi drivers give new meaning to tailgating. I'm not sure how drivers can cope when someone is right up your ass, honking their horn. After a while he pulls over, stopping in front of a hat shop – perfect. He points to the meter and I count out what I hope is enough money. The lady at the airport was nice enough to give me a quick lesson on Euros as she was exchanging my money before I left. I just hope it's enough. He doesn't say anything as I get out and pulls away before I even have the door completely shut.

It's just my suitcase and me standing at the door that should hopefully be Savannah's. I open the door and climb the stairs, quickly realizing there are multiple apartments at the top. I find her door and knock. Then I knock again and wait.

She's not home, that much is clear. I don't have anywhere to go and I'm not that eager to leave. With my back pressed against the wall, I slide down and pull my knees to my chest. Now I just have to wait.

Chapter Twenty-Four

Savannah

I don't know how much time passes before I get up and head toward the trail. Zach is nowhere to be found. I should be worried he hasn't come back, but I'm not. I deserve to be left here. If I had been honest from the beginning he could've been on the rest of his vacation instead of staying in Paris to hang out with me. Instead, the selfish Savannah played her cards, and it's coming back to bite her in the ass. Someday I'll learn. At least I hope so.

This is another reason I miss Tyler. He'd call me out on my bullshit before I get in so deep that I hurt someone else. I really need to speak with him. I need to hear his voice to fill the void that I'm feeling. I don't know what to say except I'm sorry. He's the last person I want to hurt and my radio silence is doing just that.

I pass a few people... lovers... along the path. The sight of them, arm in arm, sends pains to my heart. She's twirling a flower, one he likely picked for her along the way. Given the chance, Tyler would be like this. He's a pure southern gentleman- opening doors, pulling out stools and helping me mount my horse. I just want him doing those things in a city where we can thrive and really become a couple. Staying on the ranch is boring and mundane. Cleaning horse stalls every day and heading into town at the end of the day or eating with Aunt Sue and Uncle Bobby isn't how I want to live my life.

When I reach the bottom of the trail, Zach is there, leaning up against one of the logs with his ankles crossed. From where I'm standing, he looks peaceful. He looks like any other tourist in France, happy to be here. My approach is slow and I walk toward him head on so he can tell me to stop or move away from me. He doesn't, and I take that as a sign to sit next to him.

"Why didn't you say anything?"

Sighing heavily, I try to think of something that would make sense. Truth is, nothing does. "I don't know. We were having fun and I like hanging out with you. I figured once you leave that would be it ya know? You'd have some great memories of France to take with you and we'd never see each other again."

"You've had wine with dinner."

"The drinking age is sixteen here."

He nods as if he's forgotten that minor tidbit.

"You didn't care to know how old I am?"

Looking off toward the mountains I realize that I became so wrapped up in having a friend that it didn't matter. I was alone in New York and even though I had a bunch of friends, they were never truly people who I could just talk to. When I arrived on the ranch I held onto that attitude until Tyler and Jeremiah reminded me that they're my true friends, especially Jeremiah with his stupid nickname for me. I can't imagine any girl wants to be called Mouse, but right now I'd love to hear it.

Zach was the replacement, the one person to make me feel like I mattered here in Paris. He didn't judge me by my apartment, my mother's job, or the clothes I was wearing. I could be me and he was none the wiser. That was wrong of me though.

"I wanted to know, but we were having fun and didn't want to ruin things."

"You know I started thinking that I really don't know much about you, except that your dad died and you're from Texas and New York. I've invested my vacation in someone that I hardly know, and I did it because you made me smile and it's been so long since I've smiled. War can take its toll and while my friends are back on base seeing their wives and girlfriends, I didn't want to go home and have to say goodbye again.

"I met you on my first day here and have enjoyed every day we've been together. It didn't matter so much that I felt like I needed to know everything about you right away and I figured we'd get to know each other more over the next week or so I have left." Zach pauses, taking out his bottle of water to take a drink.

"It's not your fault," he says as he screws the lid back on. "There are things I should've asked. I think I was just too excited to meet an American, a cute one at that." Zach bumps my shoulder and my cheeks turn red.

"I'm really sorry, Zach. I didn't mean to lie to you."

He turns his head in my direction and smiles. "You didn't, but under the laws of full disclosure I think you should tell me if you have a boyfriend back home that's going to come kicking my ass."

I can't help but laugh. "I don't think he's my boyfriend and I doubt he'll want to kick your ass."

"What's his name?"

"Tyler," I tell him.

"What does he do?"

I look at him questioningly. "Why all the questions?"

Zach shrugs and takes another drink of his water. "I guess I want to know about the guy who let his girlfriend travel clear across the country and didn't go with her."

I think about this for a minute and realize I know the reasoning. I never thought to ask him to come with me. I'm not sure he would've, but I could've offered. Or at least told him what my plans are and when I'm coming back.

I take a deep breath and mentally prepare myself for a look of disgust when he sees how selfish I am. "I didn't ask him," I say honestly. "He runs my uncle's farm and works a lot. I wanted to come to Paris and figure things out. This was my plan before I even went back to Texas."

"And you didn't want him messing it up?"

"Yes," I say without reservation. "It's mean I know, but I wanted Paris before I was sent to the ranch... things changed there, but I'm not ready to change my life."

Zach reaches for my hand, clasping his fingers with mine. "It's not mean if it's the truth. It's better that you take what you need out of life now before you look back on it in ten years with regret."

He doesn't give me an opportunity to respond as he pulls me toward the tour bus we arrived on earlier. It's about a two-hour bus ride back to Paris, which could be awkward considering the topic of discussion we were having or it could be nice and quiet if we both fall asleep.

Zach has made me think more about my situation

with Tyler. We never declared ourselves a couple, which is something someone my age wants, but not necessarily something he would do. He's past all that high school "will you be my boyfriend" crap, but I'm not. My emotional state needs the hard facts, not this read between the lines stuff. What if I read the wrong thing and go one way while he goes the other?

I could already be going the other way. I haven't done any soul-searching because I've spent most of my time people watching and being a tourist. I've done nothing to figure out about University and I don't even know if I want to stay here. Being someone like Aunt Sue doesn't appeal either. I just don't know if I could live on the ranch and be happy and that's not fair to Tyler. He needs a woman who wants to be like Aunt Sue. Who doesn't mind cooking big dinners and feeding everyone on the ranch. That's just not me.

Although, right now, I'm not really sure I know who "me" is, either.

Zach shakes my shoulder just as the overhead lights turn on. I fell asleep and by the looks of it, I fell asleep on him. I yawn and stretch, looking around at the others on the bus doing the same thing. He holds my hand again as we get off the bus. It feels good. He makes me feel safe and protected. But so does Tyler. I like Zach, but he doesn't make my heart beat faster like Tyler does.

When we reach my flat, Zach pulls me into a hug. It feels good to hug him back. I fit in his arms. He kisses me on the forehead and says he'll wait for me to get to my window.

"Savannah?" he says my name before the door to my stairs closes. I push it open and smile at him. "Tomorrow, breakfast?"

"Of course." It's a relief knowing my mistakes aren't coming back to bite me in the ass. He could've just left me tonight and never looked back, but he didn't.

I take each step slowly. I'm not sore, but I'm definitely tired. Emotions take a lot out of you, more than you tend to think. I hesitate at the top of the stairs when I see a dark figure sitting in front of my door. My heart races as I eye the person and look back down the stairs. The lighting in this hallway needs to be upgraded and now would be a great time for them to do it.

The person stands and faces me. It's flight or fight time.

"Savannah?"

I cover my mouth as I half scream, half gasp. Rushing down the hall I jump into his arms and cry.

Chapter Twenty-Five

Tyler

*A*nnamae was always jumping into my arms whenever I saw her. Even if it were an hour after I dropped her off. I hated it, found it annoying and ridiculous. A few times I thought it'd be funny to not catch her, but I always did.

Savannah jumping into my arms is a relief. The way she wraps herself around me, allowing me to bury my nose in her hair and hold her to me, sends a sense of calm through my body. Coming to Paris was the right decision regardless of what happens while I'm here. Being with her right now is what we both needed.

No lie, I was scared as the day turned to night and she hadn't returned. My fears of her finding someone new or not being in town plagued my thoughts all day. I knew the risk, but was willing to take it just to see her, just to have this moment with her, even if it's my last.

When you have nothing but time to kill, you start to

158

think and that's not always a beneficial thing. Coupled with my fears, each time I heard footsteps I readied myself for rejection. I could picture her face in my head, the look of disgust and anger as she saw me standing by her door waiting.

It's still there even as I hold her close – that feeling that she doesn't want me here. I'm afraid to let her go. Afraid that the moment I let her down, and she looks at me, her face will fall and I'll be asked... no told... to leave. I don't want to hear that Paris makes her happy and I know that makes me selfish, but she's in my arms and all I want to do is carry her out of here and back to the airport.

Against my will, she wants down. I hold her as I lower her until her feet touch the ground and only then do I reluctantly loosen my grip. Her hands are soft against my face as she holds me, letting her fingers tickle the scruff growing in.

"I think I'm dreaming," she says.

I want to kiss her, but the sounds of footsteps stop me. I look over her shoulder to find a man coming toward us. Before I can acknowledge his presence Savannah's name is falling from his lips. I can't even describe what I'm feeling. My skin feels tight. My heart is racing. My tongue feels heavy as Savannah turns in my arms and takes a step toward this man. She's met someone else.

I'm too late.

"Zach?" her voice is soft and welcoming. I instantly hate that I'm here and hate the man standing on the other side of her.

"You didn't come to the window... is everything okay?" I glare at him, hoping to convey that she belongs to me. I can't help it. Savannah is worth fighting for and he needs to know that. I have a feeling this is going to be a showdown and not the Wild West kind. It'll be him versus me with Savannah in the middle. I give him a good look – noticing that he's the same stature as I am. It'll be a fair fight.

Except when Savannah turns and looks at me, I get the feeling that I've already lost. I suck in my bottom lip to bite it, anything to tell my brain that the pain is okay. She smiles, but it doesn't reach her eyes, it's nothing like I'm used to from her.

"Everything's great. I was just saying –"

"Please don't," I say as my voice breaks.

"It's not what it looks like. I promise." She grabs for my hand and I let her. If I'm stupid enough to believe those words I might as well get one last hand hold out of the deal.

Savannah looks back at her friend and all I want to do is throw her over my shoulder and start running. It's ridiculous, I know, but there's something about her that makes me want to do stupid things like profess my love to anyone that will listen. I hope this "Zach" guy doesn't feel the same way.

"Zach, this is Tyler."

He steps forward before she can finish her sentence. Or maybe she's done and I'm just hoping for more.

"Hey, man, it's nice to meet you." Before I know it, we're shaking hands and I feel like I'm in the Twilight Zone.

"Are we still on for breakfast?" he asks, as she looks back and forth between him and me.

"Let's shoot for lunch at the café on the corner." He kisses her on the cheek and disappears down the hall, all while I stand there trying to figure out what's going on.

"Hey," she says, as she places her hand against my cheek and turns me toward her. "Do you think that maybe you want to kiss me?"

"What about that guy?"

"Kiss me first and then I'll tell you."

I fight the urge to be like her and roll my eyes. "It doesn't work like that, Savvy." She sighs and leaves the confines of our personal bubble to open her door. After she steps in, I follow and take in the scene before me. The windows are long and covered by gold curtains that would make Aunt Sue cringe, with dark red furniture set against stark white walls. Everything screams "do not touch" and I can picture my mother squeezing the crap out of my hand as we walk through a store where someone would buy all of this.

"Are you thirsty or hungry?" Savannah takes my bag and sets it down against the white wall, causing me to worry that I'm too dirty to be in this place. My farm clothes are going to soil everything if I'm not careful. Talk about being uncomfortable.

"I am, but that can all wait. I want to see you. Talk to you. Just even holding you right now would be enough." I step to her, placing my hand on her hip. I let out a long exhale as I summon up the courage to ask the question that's at the forefront of my mind. "Are you in love with that guy?"

Savannah falls into me, wrapping her arms around my waist. As much as I want to kiss her, I refuse. I have to know where her heart is, even if this is the last time I see her. Her fingers move into my hair, pushing my ball cap off my head. Internally, I cringe, thinking about it dirtying up the floor when it lands but Savannah doesn't seem to care.

"No, I'm not," she whispers as her lips hover dangerously close to mine. My fingers dig into her hips as I pull her body flush with mine. "I met him a week ago. He's a Marine on leave and we've just been hanging out."

"Why was he waiting for you?"

"To make sure I made it into my apartment safely."

For some reason the words "my apartment" cause me to step back. Is she established already? Am I too late to change her mind? I move away from her to fully take in the place that she lives. That she's calling home. It's grand compared to the ranch and something I could never provide for her. It hits me like a ton of bricks just how opposite she and I are. I know from experience even love can't overcome the desire to live a different lifestyle.

"Tyler, what's wrong?"

"This," I say as I spread my hands out. "I can't compete with this."

Savannah steps behind me and rests cheek against my shoulder. It's a simple moment like this – when I realize how well we fit – that kills me knowing we likely won't end up together. I can see it now, in five or ten years from now, she'll come back and if we're both single we'll hookup because the attraction is there, but I have a feeling that's all we'll end up being.

"Do you want to compete with it?"

Turning in her arms, I grab her face and bring our lips together. Our kiss starts off slowly and is nothing but lips until her hands pull my hair. I let Savannah lead. I let her dictate where this kiss is going. She whimpers as her tongue touches mine and her nails dig into my scalp. My mind is racing, battling with my heart as my hands roam over her body grasping to hold every inch of her.

She pulls away all too soon, leaving me aching for

more. Her fingers move in and out of my hair as she labors her breathing, pressing her forehead to mine as she gives me a lingering kiss before sighing. "I've missed you so much."

Those words are the ones I've been dying to hear, but didn't realize how much they'd tear at my heart. I want to get down on bended knee and profess my love, but it's too soon, and she has a lot of life to live before she's tied down. Besides, I may not be enough. I want to be enough, though, and know I may need to change for her in order to accomplish that. Can I give up the ranch and be the man she wants me to be?

I'm not sure. The ranch is all I know. It's all I've cared about for years. It's in my blood and was once in hers.

"You have no idea how happy I am that you're here."

"Tell me," I beg her. If she's willing to open up, I'm more than willing to absorb everything she wants to tell me.

She takes my hand, stopping to pick up my hat. She places it on my head awkwardly but I don't dare fix it. I steal a kiss before I bend over to pick up my suitcase and let her lead me wherever she's taking me. I wonder if she knows that I'd follow her anywhere. Evident by the fact that I'm so out of my comfort zone, I feel like I'm having an out of body experience. I'm out of my element, yet so at ease as long as I'm with Savannah.

We walk down the hall and into her room. It's vastly different from the living room, but still too fashionable for my tastes. Many different kinds of fabrics cover the walls and drape over the window. Soft, muted light flows through giving off a moonlight ambience.

"This is nice."

She shrugs. "It's whatever. There's something missing though."

"What's that?" I ask, as I set my bag and hat down. Her fingers trail up my arm, resting on my shoulders.

"You," she whispers against my lips.

Chapter Twenty-Six

Savannah

*P*inch me.
        Pinch me again.
Pinch me again and again.

The boy... no he's so much more than a boy... the man that makes my heart beat a little bit faster, who makes my palms sweat, who makes my skin tingle, is standing in my bedroom in Paris. If I didn't know better, I'd say it's a dream. But my dream wouldn't include Zach coming back to shake Tyler's hand. That's how I knew Tyler was real. That's how I knew he was here for me.

And now with him standing in my room, I want nothing more than to be with him, to fall asleep in his arms and to hold his hand while we tour Paris and he falls in love. Except, he's not here to sightsee or fall in love with our surroundings. Even I know that. The proverbial elephant sitting in the corner with its trunk in the air is reminding me of that. But my plan is to ignore everything and just live in the moment. I don't want to know when he's going home or what he's really doing here. Those answers will come in due time. Right now, its just Tyler, me, and the city I've fallen in love with.

He looks around my room. It's different from the one I have in Texas, but a lot like the one I had in New York. I found the tapestries at a farmers market during my first weekend here. I had to have them and loved stopping at every stand that I went to that day. I didn't do those things in Texas. I barely left the ranch. I don't know why, either. I was either afraid or just not willing to unless it was to a mall, but when I arrived here and came upon the market, it felt right. It's what I wanted to do. It's what I imagine myself doing every weekend.

"This is what I'm like," I tell him as I let the fabric run over my fingers. "In New York I decorated my room with art, tapestries and lights." I walk over to the other side of my room, which is just a fabric-covered wall. "At my mom's, this wall had a bookshelf on it. I would look through second-hand stores for old books. Chaucer, Bronte... anything I could find."

"Did you ever read them?"

I shake my head as my fingers move along the wall. Tyler needs to know this about me. He needs to know the real me. Not the girl that was sent to her Uncle's ranch for breaking the rules. Not the girl who wore cowboy boots and cleaned horse stalls. That wasn't me.

"No time," I tell him. "There were parties and social gatherings that had to be attended. Shopping had to be done. Teachers didn't care about our homework, just who our parents were. The firm my mom works for, they're the legal council for the school so I had a free pass. A bunch of us did. There was the Senator's daughter, the CEO's son. It didn't matter as long as the school saw the money.

"So we partied, and we went to clubs. Everyone slept late on Saturdays except for me. I'd wake up and take the train out of town while all my friends slept it off. I'd find a farmer's market and just spend hours and hours looking at everything. My mother hated everything I brought back and so did my friends," I trail off. He knows about my so-called friends. The moment shit went south they bailed and acted like they didn't know me.

"I like your room. It's different, but I like it."

"It's me. The pink room with the box full of My Little Ponies isn't me. I'm sure it could've been had I never moved, but New York is so cultural, so diverse. One week-end, I sat in Central Park and listened to an African band play for hours. I just sat there and when I got home my mom was livid because the maid hadn't shown up yet and she needed coffee." I laugh even though it's not funny. If the maid wasn't there, it was my responsibility to keep her focused on her job and if that meant she needed coffee, I was to get it for her.

"You could –"

"Don't say it," I say, as I step in front of him and put my fingers to his lips. "I don't want to talk about why you're here. I just want to be with you. I just want to hold you, touch you." My fingers trail down the front of his shirt pulling each button. "Tomorrow I want to be like those other couples I see at the Eiffel Tower, kissing in the sunset. Can you give me that?"

"I'll give you anything you ask for, Savannah," Tyler says as he walks us backwards toward my bed. "I think you know that." He stops when I fall onto my bed. He finishes unbuttoning his shirt, rolling it over each shoulder one at a time. His sculptured chest beckons as I let my lips press against this skin.

Tyler lifts my chin, pulling me away from him. "Where's the lady you live with?"

I sit back on my bed and pull him with me. We both lay on our sides facing each other. I have to put a pillow between us because his chest is distracting and I need to focus on him and not his body.

"When I left you at the airport, I wanted to turn around. I wanted to go back to you and ask you to take me away. It didn't matter where, just away from Texas, New York, even here, but I knew you wouldn't leave the ranch and I could never bring myself to be selfish enough to ask. So I got on the plane because that's what my mother wanted.

"When I arrived, I was in the city I had only dreamt about...the city I wanted to be in even though I had only seen it through pictures. My first weekend, as you know, was everything I thought it would be. But then the work-week came around and Alexis disappeared. She works more than my mother does and I never see her. I'm alone again at dinner and on weekends, left to figure life out on my own."

I'm ruining Tyler's surprise with my less than stellar parental life. I can see the anguish in his eyes as he keeps eye contact with me. His touch is soft as he pushes my hair behind my ear. I turn slightly and kiss his palm as it rests on my cheek.

"What are your dreams now, Savannah?"

I close my eyes as tears start to flow. He's my dream, but I'm not ready. I'm not yet eighteen and have always said I don't want to end up like my mother. What if I grew to resent Tyler when he's been nothing but good to me? I'm not sure I'd be able to live with myself.

Then there's the ranch. He loves it. I outgrew it. One

of us would have to make a sacrifice and I'm not sure I can do that.

"I'm not sure my dreams are worthy of what dreams should be," I tell him.

"Everyone's dreams should be followed."

"What if they hurt the ones you love?"

He knows what I'm talking about and doesn't pull away knowing that we could end here. "If you love someone, you let them follow their dreams and hope that eventually their dreams lead them back to you."

"When did you get so smart?"

"I'm not Savannah, I'm just scared of losing you forever, so I'm willing to let you go in hopes you'll come back to me in the end." Tyler trails his hand down my side until it's gripping my hip. "I know we're different, but we haven't always been. I know I can make you happy if you give me the chance."

"And what if I can't make you happy?"

"Impossible," he says, as he kisses my nose.

"Tyler..."

He stops what I'm about to say by sealing my lips with his. The pillow separating us is thrown across the room and before I can catch my breath I'm under him. Tyler pulls away, but not before grinding into me.

"I didn't want you to think I came here just for sex, but I've missed you too much and seeing you... well, shit, I'm going to sound like Jeremiah here and tell you that you're just too damn hot and I'm horny as hell."

I can't help but laugh. "So what you're saying is you like me?" I ask, thrusting back.

"A little more than like," he says as he leans back on his knees, pulling me with him. He pulls at the hem of my shirt, bringing it over my head and unclasping my bra as soon as my shirt is off.

"More than like?"

"Mhm," he mumbles as he places kisses over my breasts. He looks at me as he pulls away. "I'm in love with you Savannah. I've been in love with you since before I knew what love was. I'm so in love with you that I'll do anything you ask of me."

"Is that so?"

Tyler nods, pulling his t-shirt up and over his head. His abs are on full display and much more defined than I remember. I can't resist the urge to touch them as my finger starts to trace each curve, valley and dip along his abdomen.

"You've been working out?" I look up quickly, waiting for an answer to my question.

Tyler nods again. "I have nothing but time on my hands right now."

My finger stops at his belt for a brief second before I give it a tug. As soon as it's free, it dangles there, the metal pieces clanking against each other and echoing throughout my room.

"We should turn on some music and lock the door."

Tyler agrees and goes to the door while I turn on my iPod. The music is classical, and he looks at me questioningly. I raise my eyebrow and eye his pants before looking back at him. He laughs and slowly unbuttons his jeans, one painstakingly slow button at a time. I swallow when his bulge pushes through from its own eagerness to come out.

"You have... um, quite the package there," I say, barely able to spit it out before I start to laugh.

"What the... have you been secretly talking to Jeremiah?" he asks, as he shimmies out of his jeans. He stands there in front me, clad only in boxer briefs with his hands on his hips. "I think you need to get undressed."

He grabs my ankles, pulling me toward him. I giggle, but quickly use my hand to cover my mouth. Even though Alexis isn't home, the last thing I want is for our neighbors to say they heard noises coming from my room. Instead of taking my shorts off, he kisses my bare stomach, moving softly along the waistband and around my belly button sending a spark of fire right to where I want him... where I need him.

I clumsily work at getting my shorts off while Tyler's mouth makes love to my stomach. He has me moving any which way to get him to move south. He smiles, teasing me with his tongue. I sigh loudly when I feel his fingers grip the sides of my underwear, swiftly taking them off before he removes his own.

Tyler moves toward me, causing me to back up. He hovers, his naked body lining up with mine.

"Sometimes I think I'm dreaming when I look at you."

"Why would you say that?" I ask cupping his cheek and letting my fingertips play with his hair.

His answer comes in the form of a kiss, a deep pene- trating one that lets me feel what he means. My fingers tangle in his hair as our tongues move against each other. My legs spread, inviting him to center himself, showing him that I want this. Tyler rocks on his knees, the tip of his erection rubbing against my clit. Even the lightest sensation is causing the heat to rise in my body. Instinct causes my hips to buck. Knowing he's so close is unbear- able. I grip his cock, stroking him as he moves above me.

Tyler tugs at my lip when I set him at my core. His eyes meet mine asking if I'm ready. He should know that

I'm ready for anything when it comes to him. Someday I'll be able to tell him that, but until then, I can show him that he has every part of me. I raise my hips, meeting him half way.

The gentle way he presses into me causes my back to arch. Tyler pulls out, only to enter again. He feels weightless against my skin as he sets our rhythm, pumping in and out. The annoying squeak of my mattress is a turn on and I dig my nails into his lower back, pushing him harder into me.

Tyler peppers me with kisses as our slick bodies move against each other. He hitches my leg over his shoulder, changing positions. Our tempo increases, the pressure building for me as he picks up the pace. My leg is dropped, and he rears back on his knees, gripping my hips to meet his thrusts.

I scream out, with a stern reminder to be quiet, but that doesn't last when he rubs my sensitive clit. My headboard slams against the wall, for sure alerting the neighbors of what's going on. Right now I don't care because the tightening of my walls around his cock is the best feeling ever.

"Savannah... shit... oh fuck..." his words are said breathlessly as he dives into me without reservation. I take all of him as he lands on me, pounding hard until he's reached his release. He moans, twitching with an aftershock while he kisses my shoulder and neck.

"I'm not trying to ruin the moment, but I think that was better than our first time."

"Every time with you is like our first time," I tell him with a kiss. We're going to have to have a lot of first times before he leaves. They're going to need to be enough until I see him again.

Chapter Twenty-Seven

Tyler

*C*owboys don't belong in Paris or maybe they do and I just need to find a way to fit in. After one of the best night's sleep I've had in a long time, I'm a tourist. This is only after we had to stop and buy me some decent tennis shoes to compensate for the amount of walking we're doing today. Savannah said as comfortable as my boots are, they're no match for the streets of Paris. She would know by the way she's dragging me around.

We slept in, or at least that's what I assumed until she begged me not to make a peep. She was waiting for Alexis to leave before we got up to start our day. It pained me to think I put her in that position and suggested that I get a hotel for the remainder of the week. She refused, saying she wasn't leaving my side. I really want her to remember that when I get on a plane and she's left standing there, waving goodbye. She knows it doesn't have to be like this.

Meeting Zach for lunch wasn't high on my list of things to do, but after spending an hour or so with him I'm pleased that Savannah had him to hang out with. This is his last day in Paris and as he told Savannah so, I watched for any sign that I was, in fact, intruding on something between them. There weren't any, much to my relief. As much as I hate to admit it, there was a nagging feeling inside telling me she wanted to be with him. He's far worldlier than I am.

And now we stand on a cobblestone path surrounded by Claude Monet's flowers. We toured the do-not-touch-anything-house and marveled at all his paintings just like the other tourists next to me. I'm a simple guy and honestly don't get it. He painted some pictures, they're nice, but to have your house turned into a museum seems to be a bit much. Of course, if this were John Wayne's house, I'd be happier than a pig in shit. I'm slowly learning that I have to give in order to take from her and right now I'd give her the damn world if it meant she'd come home with me.

Broaching the subject of returning to Texas ain't going to be an easy one. The timing has to be right and I have to make sure not to ruin anything special she has planned. This is where I wish I had Jeremiah's courage. He'd blurt it and not worry about the consequences. Maybe that's why he doesn't do relationships. He's not the tiptoe around type of guy. Maybe that's why we get along so well.

"Aren't the flowers so pretty?"

The dumbass cowboy in me wants to say they're nothing but flowers. It's not like this Monet dude created the flower. He just painted them. And not even the ones we're looking at since those are long gone. But I can't. That would be insensitive and I'd probably insult the people around us. So I squeeze her hand and smile. "They're beautiful."

Are they? As I look around I see people taking their pictures in front of them, all smiling and happy except this one lady who is standing there looking like she's about to die. She sneezes, not once or twice, but consecutively for something like ten times in a row. Her face is red, puffy, and she looks irritated. I'm thinking that it's allergy season for her and this probably isn't the best place to be.

Savannah and I follow along with the tour guide, who is speaking English but not a version I've ever heard before. Every other word is French, or some self made word because he can't remember the English equivalent. Listening to him makes me realize that if Savannah and I are to be together and she wants to travel, we must visit English-speaking countries because I want to learn about what I'm seeing.

I pay attention when Savannah asks a question and make mental notes to plant flowers around my house. When I start thinking about my house, I start thinking that I could make it a home for her. Put up a fence, build an addition and maybe plant some trees for privacy. The thought of her living across the way at her Aunt and Uncle's is nice, but I want her with me. She'll be eighteen soon, she can do whatever she wants. I'm praying that whatever that is, she's considering having me be a part of it. The five-year age difference is nothing to me now. It's just a number. Just like the years that kept us apart.

Making her life better is what I want to be able to do for her. Savannah needs a family. She needs to know and feel like people care about her. Her mother took that away from her when they left Texas. The promises of visits never happened, and we were soon missing everything going on in her life. If they had visited, I don't think she and I would be in Paris right now. Or maybe we would, and I wouldn't be worrying about how I'm going to convince her to come home with me.

We follow the crowd back to the bus, except we don't get on it. We didn't actually pay for the guided tour; we sort of just blended in. And while they'll get a comfortable ride to their next stop, we're heading back to Paris on the train. I actually don't mind. Walking alone, with only Savannah to occupy my mind is perfect.

I never thought I'd want to be in love again after Annamae. Everything that she did gave me pause. Annamae convinced me that I could live both lives: the rancher and the socialite's husband. Being away from her during the week is what led her to start lying and cheating. Rufus was there, weaseling his way into my role in her life. I should thank him because I have a feeling I would've been the one to lie and cheat the moment I laid eyes on Savannah.

I always thought my mom was crazy with her "You're meant to be with Savannah" talk. This came up every time Annamae would mention marriage. My mom didn't like her, but she loves Savannah, even if she hasn't seen her in years.

There's a field of flowers along our walk and even though it's probably illegal, I stop and pick one.

"What are you doing?" Savannah looks up and down the road for oncoming vehicles, but can't hide her giggle.

"Well, as we've been walking and looking at flowers all morning I realized that something has been missing." I slide the white and pink flower, the kind I have no idea what it is, into her hair just behind her ear.

"What if this is part of Monet's garden?"

I look around and shrug. "So what? He's long gone and won't miss a single flower. Besides, it was screaming at me that it needed to be in your hair."

"It was, huh?" Her hands fist my shirt as she brings me closer.

"It was. I know it's not possible, but you're even more stunning with this little flower in your hair. Your eyes are brighter and your cheeks are pinker." I want to immediately take back every stupid cheesy thing I just said. That's not me. I can talk about tractors, hay and horses. I'm not romantic. It's likely my downfall, but looking at Savannah now tells me I'm wrong. The adoration in her eyes is telling me everything I just said is right.

"Tyler... you make me feel special and wanted." Her eyes glisten, making me feel like crap.

"Don't cry."

"Happy tears, I promise." Her lips press against mine as images of rolling around in the field behind us tease me of what could be if we were home.

"What's next on our list?"

"The Eiffel Tower. I want to hold you with the clouds behind us and the lights of the tower illuminating us while we kiss."

"Then off to the tower we must go!"

Chapter Twenty-Eight

Savannah

*T*he sun is setting and I'm on the second floor of the Eiffel Tower again, this time with the man that I love. He's standing next me, letting the breeze blow through his hair. I take out my phone and snap a quick picture while his eyes are closed. Not only do I plan to look at it repeatedly, but I also want to show him that he once did have fun in a foreign country.

In order to show him I need to be with him. Thinking that in a few short days he'll be leaving Paris and I'll still be here isn't sitting well. I'm here at least until I turn eighteen. I can't up and leave without an issue. Once I have my birthday, I fully plan to exercise my right of choice by doing something for me. I don't know what that is at this time though. I love being far away from my mother and my life back in New York. I didn't fall in love with the ranch, but I fell in love with Tyler. Finding a happy medium is going to be a challenge.

A commotion behind us causes Tyler to turn and

stand in front of me. He's been well versed on how heavy the crime is here, especially in the tourist spots. After he realizes it's nothing, he turns back, wrapping me in his arms.

"I've come to the conclusion that leading a life as a criminal is the best way to make a living in Paris."

"Is that so?"

"It is. The way I see it, you're beautiful and could totally distract my unsuspecting victim while I clean them out good. We can hit a spot every few days then go on the run. Come back with a disguise or something. I wouldn't want the police force to catch on to our ruse."

"Our ruse? I don't know about that, Tyler. It sounds more like you're using me." Leaning up on my tiptoes I kiss him and let my lips linger against his. He's only been here a day and my mind has spent a majority of our time together in the gutter. Not that I'm sharing my thoughts, even though I know he'll appreciate them. We definitely didn't have enough time together before I had to leave and he can't stay in my room his whole time here. Uncle Bobby and Aunt Sue are expecting pictures and stories of his time in France, I'm sure.

"You wouldn't be the Bonnie to my Clyde?"

I angle my head and pretend to think about this offer. He tickles me when I don't answer right away.

"Tyler, I don't know how I feel about leading a life of crime. Isn't there something else we could do?"

His face gets serious. I'm afraid I've opened Pandora's Box now. We have to have a conversation and it's one that I don't want to even think about. A simple life is what I want, but he won't allow it. I could go on, living like the invisible person I am, except Tyler wants me to shine and brighten everything around him.

"Where are we going next?" As much as I wanted to wait until it was dark, he's right. We should leave and find a place to discuss us and any future we might have. Taking his hand in mine I lead him back to the elevator. We cram in like sardines as we descend to the bottom.

Since I told Tyler about the high rate of pickpockets in the city, he's on high alert. The shoulder bumping, the people suddenly falling in front of you and even the lame attempt to get your attention has him walking closer to me, ready to protect if given the chance.

"I'm afraid I'm going to punch someone."

"Do it. The police won't care. I doubt they'll even get the hint. I've seen some tourists fight with them and the police just sit there."

"I know I'm from the country and don't get out much, but this is crazy. They're like mosquitos."

"Yeah I guess they are." I hadn't though of them like that, but he's right. It doesn't matter how hard you hit them, they keep coming back for more.

We walk along the Seine. My head rests on his shoulder and our hands are clasped together. This is what I've dreamt about. Being in Paris and being in love. The city is magical and you can't help but fall for it.

Tyler directs us to a bench and we sit down. He angles his body so he can look at me and I know... this is the talk. Not that I've been dreading it. I just didn't want it to happen.

"Paris is beautiful, Savannah."

"You haven't even seen all of it yet." I remind him if only to earn more time before he blurts out the words I don't want to hear.

"I'm trying not to be that guy. I'm trying to let everything happen naturally, but now that I'm here and holding you in my arms, I have to know. Or maybe I don't have to know and I'm just telling myself I do because hearing the words will either make or break this trip for me. What do you want Savannah?"

I breathe in deeply. He's asking the same question I've been asking myself for months. It's easy to say that I want Tyler. I know for a fact I want him in my life, but how and in what capacity can we make it work? Knowing the answer to that question would solve the "what ifs" plaguing my mind.

"Before I answer, know that I love you. You need to know that you're the most important person in my life and the only one who is willing to let me grow up and be who I want to be. With that said, I don't know who I want to be. I think being back in Texas reminded me that life used to be so simple. You get up, you work, you play and you enjoy your family. New York didn't work like that, at least not for me. Right now, I resent my mom for taking me away from you, your mom, Aunt Sue and Uncle Bobby. Hell even Jeremiah. I missed so much, but I've also been afforded an opportunity to live here."

I spread my arms out, and he looks around, listening to what I have to say. I'm not sure if it makes sense, but he's paying attention. He's giving me the freedom to speak my mind without judgment.

"There are two things for certain: One, I want to be with you. Two, I want to go to school. Now whether that is here, or in Texas or some other state, I don't know. My fear is that if I tell my mother that I want to be in Texas, she's going to stop paying for me and I don't know what I'd do. I can't ask Uncle Bobby for money and short of mucking stalls, I don't have any work experience."

Tyler takes my hand in his and relaxes against the

bench. "I've done a lot of thinking since you left. I know you're too young to settle down and I also know you don't want to live on the ranch."

I start to shake my head but the look in his eyes makes me stop.

"I can accept that we're different, Savannah, and it's okay. What I want to tell you is this... I want you to come back to Texas and move in with my momma. She says you can live there and go to school. I'll come up on the weekends if you want me to, and we'll try having a relationship. If your mom cuts you off, I'll help pay for school."

"Tyler – "

"Listen, please. We want you home, Savvy. The short time you were on the ranch changed things. You're the beacon - or something like that - according to Aunt Sue and she misses you. So even if you're only there for the weekends or holidays, we want you to come home.

"And I want to be with you. I want to take my girl to the honkytonk and two-step with her on a Saturday night. I want to hold you by the bonfire and make love to you under the stars. Hell, right about now I'd get down on my knee and ask you to be my wife, but I'm not ready for that."

The thought of marriage doesn't scare me, but being married at eighteen does.

"What's stopping you?"

Tyler smiles and his eyes light up. My stomach starts to turn, thinking that I've said something I shouldn't have.

"Me. I'm stopping me. I want to build a house for us. Plant some flowers and make it a real home. Sure it's cozy now, but you deserve more. Plus, I want you to go school and experience life. You have to make sure living on a ranch is something you want to do."

"And what if it's not?" I throw that out there for him to ponder. He's a rancher, not me. What if I can't live on the ranch without going stir crazy and pulling my hair out like my mother?

"Then we'll move somewhere in between and I'll commute. I'm not losing you again, Savannah McGuire."

Chapter Twenty-Nine

Tyler

I'm not losing you again, Savannah McGuire.

Those words have replayed over and over in my thoughts every day since I left Paris without her. It's been two months, and each day feels longer than the next. The calls are sporadic at best. The time difference makes it difficult, as well as my long hours, but we try. The emails are more frequent and I've started hounding the high-speed internet companies to move their fiber optics lines out this way for better access. For now, it's slow, but worth it just to see her email in the morning. However the fact of the matter is, she's still in Paris and I'm back on the ranch.

Nothing was resolved before I left. Not that I expected it be. One thing that did happen is that she had a nice long talk with my mom about coming back to Texas and moving in with her. I think this is what Savannah needs - a mother who is going to take care of her and let her grow. I thought for sure she'd be flying back with me, but no such luck. Pressuring her will only backfire so I'm patient. I'm told she'll make a decision soon and Jeremiah wants to know how long I'm willing to wait. He doesn't get it. His constant one night stand marathon through the hearts of Texas may work for him, but not for me. What he doesn't know is I'd probably wait forever.

Savannah is going through a tough time. She's a girl who deserves to be loved fully and appreciated for who she is. Her mother has taken away that connection and, because of that, it's hard for her to accept that people care about her without having ulterior motives. Her friends in New York used her and when shit went south they bailed, acting as if she did something wrong. Jeremiah would never do that. If I were to go down in flames, he'd be right there with me. Savannah needs someone like Jeremiah in her life, preferably a female if it ain't me. Not that I'd be jealous or anything.

Who am I kidding? I'd be freaking beside myself if I had to share her with anyone. Even the brief moment in Paris when Zach was standing there, acting protective over her, I thought I had lost her and would have to fight and crawl my way back into her life. As much as I hate to admit it, Zach would be a good friend to her... or an older, wiser brother-type, which she could use. Someone who would protect her if need be and be there for her when the time came.

Pulling the tractor into the barn, I shut it off and sit there for minute in the quiet. Everyone has gone home early to get ready for Uncle Bobby's surprise birthday party. Aunt Sue and my mother got it in their heads that Bobby needed a party. I told them they're crazy if they think he's gonna enjoy himself at Red's, but they didn't listen. Somehow Aunt Sue was able to take Bobby away from the ranch for the day, too. That knocked me back a few steps when he said he was taking the day off. With him being gone, I didn't have to suffer his wrath when I let people out early. Most of the crew will be at Red's to wish him a happy birthday and at least they'll have time to shower first.

As soon as I pull into my driveway, Jeremiah is there, sitting on the tailgate of his truck.

"What are you doing here so early?"

He shrugs and jumps down, following me into my house. On the coffee table are the plans I've drawn up to expand. I try to pick them up before he can see them but I'm too late.

"What's this?"

I sigh, taking off my hat and tossing it onto the chair on the other side of my living room. "I'm going to build an addition."

"Why?"

Sitting down, I take the plans from his hand. After coming back from Paris I decided that even if Savannah isn't with me, I needed to expand. I can't live in a small house for the rest of my life and I may want a family some day. Might as well do this while I have the time.

"I'm going to make it like Bobby and Sue's place."

Jeremiah shakes his head. "What if she never comes back?"

I rub my hands down my legs before standing. Over the past few months I've done a lot of pacing when I'm not sleeping or at work.

"I still need to do it. This is my home and I need to invest in my future."

Jeremiah picks up the drawings again before setting them down. "Man, you've got it hard for a chick that ain't even here. What if you do all of this and she never comes back, or she does but shows up with a boyfriend?"

She won't do that because she loves me. I don't say that to him, though, because he'll never understand.

I shrug in return. "Well I'll have a nice house for a nice girl when the time comes." I leave him there while I go take a shower. It's quick because we have to get to Red's, but the longer I let the water run the clearer my thoughts are. In a way, he's right. She's not here, yet I'm planning for a future with her. Not enough time has passed for me to give up on her. I don't have a predetermined time limit, but a few months ain't enough.

Jeremiah won't let me hang on too long though. He's too good of a friend to let me live in limbo. It's not going to matter how hard I try.

WHEN WE ARRIVE at Red's the parking lot is full and over flowing and we have to park down the street. I know Bobby is well respected, but I never thought he'd pack the house at the local bar. It's been a long time since I've seen this many cars here. It'll be a good night for Della tending bar.

Jeremiah rushes ahead of me, probably hoping that one of his flames is there. Sometimes I wonder why I even come out with him. He could at least walk with me into the bar.

For being so packed, it's sure quiet on the outside. I can't hear any music playing and am assuming Bobby has asked them to turn it down. That would be embarrassing for Sue, but Bobby is known to be a curmudgeon.

I pull the wooden door open and step in. It takes a moment for my eyes to adjust to the darkness.

"Surprise!" Many voices yell as the lights come on. I stand there with my mouth gaping open like a fish searching for water. My mom comes up to me and gives me a hug. I barely recognize that her arms are around me and forget to hug her back.

"What is this?"

"It's an early birthday party. We wanted to surprise you."

"Well, I'm definitely surprised."

My birthday isn't for another month and before I can ask who she's talking about with her "we", a beer is being pushed into my hand and birthday wishes are given. Then I'm pushed into the middle of the dance floor where a giant birthday cake sits on the floor.

"There better be a naked chick in there," Jeremiah says loud enough for everyone to hear. I shake my head and meet the gazes of Bobby and Sue who both look mortified. Great. Here I am telling them that I'll take care of their niece and my best friend is hoping there's a naked woman inside my cake.

The tall candles are lit and everyone starts to sing. I step forward and take a deep breath in.

"Don't forget to make a wish," someone yells.

I smile and thank them, inhaling again to blow out the candles. As soon as they're out, cheers erupt and I find myself blushing at all the unnecessary attention.

"What'd you wish for?" my mom asks, as she squeezes me cheeks. She knows. I don't need to tell her.

"You know."

"Yes, but I want to hear you say it."

"Maybe later," I tell her as I give her a kiss on the cheek.

Jeremiah hands me a knife and tells me to cut the cake. Of course, he'd be hungry.

As soon as I step up to the cake, it moves.

"What the hell?" I step forward and touch it. The frosting is hard, and doesn't seem at all edible.

"What's going on?" I ask the people surrounding me, but no one answers. Before I can ask again, my cake is exploding, much to Jeremiah's delight.

And much to mine, as well, as Savannah is standing in front of me surrounded by my very apparent cardboard cake.

"Happy Birthday," she yells as she throws her hands up in the air.

I'm too stunned to move, my jaw dropping open in complete surprise, but that doesn't stop her. Before I can comprehend that she's standing here, in Red's, her arms are wrapped around my waist.

"Am I dreaming?"

"Not at all," she says, shaking her head. "Your mom and I have been planning this for a while now. I've been back in Texas for three days."

"What?" I ask, incredulously.

"I needed to surprise you. Show you how much you mean to me."

I take this opportunity to kiss her until Jeremiah says something about the lack of cake. I laugh against her lips and quickly pull her out of the bar. We need to talk and it needs to be done without an audience.

As soon as we're outside, I push her up against the wall. I've missed her so much it hurts.

"How long are you here for?"

"Forever, if you'll have me."

"What does that mean?" My words are pleading. I have to know.

"It means that I'm back in Texas. It also means I'm still not sure if I want to stay here forever, but I do know that I want to be with you."

I tuck her hair behind her ear, and kiss her lightly. "I want nothing more."

She clutches my shirt, kissing me back with enough force that it causes me to step back. "You do want more."

I shrug and give her a half smile. I'm a guy. She's hot. That combination alone equals dirty thoughts.

"I know you want me to live with you."

"I do, but we have time for that, Savannah. I'm just happy that you're here."

Tears start to form in her eyes, reminding me that this girl needs to be loved and told so every day. If she's giving me the opportunity, I'm going to take it.

"I want to live with you, Tyler. After you left, my mom sent me a box of stuff and inside was some letters that my dad and she exchanged. They were so in love and didn't care what anyone said. He talked about you and how you'd be a stand-up guy some day and had no doubt that you'd fall in love with me.

"I'm not saying we need to get married or anything like that, but maybe we can live together and see if we're meant to be. I'll commute to the community college, take some classes until I know what I want to do and at night, we'll be together. Living a life on the ranch."

Words are caught in my throat as I listen to her say everything. If I weren't touching her, I'd think this was all a dream. But she's here, in the flesh, pouring her heart out to me.

"Yeah?" is the only response I can form, and I hate myself for being an idiot.

"Yeah," she replies as she smiles bright. "You and I, together, forever."

When I was told to make a wish, it was about Savannah. I'm not going to tell anyone what it was, but I will say this – always wish before you blow out your candles.

Read other books by Heidi McLaughlin

Acknowledgments

Thank you, thank you, thank you: Yvette, Traci, Tammy, Amy, Veronica, Audrey, Georgette, Tammy and Kelli for your constant support, guidance, patience and understanding.

Special shout-out & thank you to Stephanie Horton for loaning me your very cute accent!

The Beaumont Daily: You guys rock!

Thanks to Sarah Hansen for my gorgeous cover!

Thanks to EM Tippetts (Emily & Crew) for making everything fancy and functional.

To the readers: If you're reading this, thank you! I appreciate you turning each page and coming back for more!

About Heidi McLaughlin

Heidi McLaughlin is a New York Times, Wall Street Journal, and USA Today Bestselling author of The Beaumont Series, The Boys of Summer, and The Archers.

Originally, from the Pacific Northwest, she now lives in picturesque Vermont, with her husband, two daughters, and their three dogs.

In 2012, Heidi turned her passion for reading into a full-fledged literary career, writing over twenty novels, including the acclaimed Forever My Girl.

When writing isn't occupying her time, you can find her sitting courtside at either of her daughters' basketball games.

Heidi's first novel, Forever My Girl, has been adapted into a motion picture with LD Entertainment and Roadside Attractions, starring Alex Roe and Jessica Rothe, and opened in theaters on January 19, 2018.

Don't miss more books by Heidi McLaughlin! Sign up for her newsletter, or join the fun in her fan group!

Connect with Heidi!
www.heidimclaughlin.com

Lost in You

Lost in Us

THE BOYS OF SUMMER

Third Base

Home Run

Grand Slam

THE REALITY DUET

Blind Reality

Twisted Reality

SOCIETY X

Dark Room

Viewing Room

Play Room

THE CLUTCH SERIES

Roman

STANDALONE NOVELS

Stripped Bare

Blow

Sexcation

Santa's Secret